G000026383

the

Key of
the Tower

the

Key of

the Tower

a novel

GILBERT ADAIR

Secker & Warburg
London

Published by Secker & Warburg 1997

2 4 6 8 10 9 7 5 3 1

Copyright © Gilbert Adair 1997

First published in Great Britain in 1997 by
Secker & Warburg
Random House, 20 Vauxhall Bridge Road,
London SW1V 2SA

Random House Australia (Pty) Limited
20 Alfred Street, Milsons Point, Sydney,
New South Wales 2061, Australia

Random House New Zealand Limited
18 Poland Road, Glenfield,
Auckland 10, New Zealand

Random House South Africa (Pty) Limited
Endulini, 5A Jubilee Road, Parktown 2193, South Africa

Random House UK Limited Reg. No. 954009

A CIP catalogue record for this book
is available from the British Library

ISBN 0 436 20429 0

Papers used by Random House UK Limited are natural,
recyclable products made from wood grown in sustainable forests.
The manufacturing processes conform to the environmental
regulations of the country of origin.

Typeset by Deltatype Limited, Birkenhead, Merseyside
Printed and bound in Great Britain by
Mackays of Chatham PLC

for Ronald Bergan,
without whom

It was an object both simple and strange: a purple cube with, in the dead centre of one of its six surfaces, a switch; near that switch, and as if clamped on to the cube, the life-sized plastic simulacrum of a human hand. When you pressed the switch, a whirring noise would issue from inside the cube, the plastic hand would slowly creep forward and press the switch off again. Oh, it was a devilish thing.

Pierre Mac Orlan, *A l'ombre du grand panama jaune*

Thwaack-thwaack-thwaack-thwaack-thwaack-thwaack-thwaack.

They were starting to mesmerise me, the mechanical wipers of my squat, sallow-yellow, second-hand Mini, as they traced and retraced, clockwise and counter-clockwise, two overlapping arcs across the windscreen and contrived not quite, never quite, to jam in the middle. They were starting to remind me of nothing so much as a brace of trapeze artists on a preliminary dry run, describing two graceful, asynchronous parabolae out into the circus tent's cottony cosmos and back again, out again and back again, always just about to collide in midair yet always, always, falling short of each other. The very sound they made was mesmerising – uncannily, the dull and knobbly squeak produced by the rubbing of an outwardly spiralling disc of visibility into a rime-encrusted window pane. And in those heartbreaking instants when the windscreen had been wiped clear, and before a brand new rash of raindrops erupted, it would come as a slight but real surprise, it would even obscurely disappoint me, that the scenery hadn't meanwhile been shifted and that the dark mute road in front of me remained unaltered, with only an occasional signpost, preternaturally aglow in the gloom, to attest that I had made any headway.

The late afternoon was fantastically hued. Suspecting that I might after all have got lost, I drew my green Michelin map from the glove compartment and clumsily unfolded Brittany over my lap. Careful, careful. I scrutinised the road, the map, the road again, the map again. The last town had been Saint-Michel-des-Loups, the next was Champeux. So far, so good. With the deftness of a goose filing its feathers away in chronological order, I folded, double-folded, triple-folded the map, restored it to its cosy cubby hole in the dashboard and let the loose fingers of my right hand enact a merry little drum solo on the steering wheel's furry sheath.

I squinted at my watch. It was an inexpensive, black-dialled, metal-braceleted affair with as many useless bonuses as a boy scout's penknife. Six-forty-five. Here comes Champeux, right on cue. Exit Champeux.

I was on that dark mute road again. The rain was pouring down as heavily as ever. A storm was gathering and I heard a crack of thunder directly over my head. Beadlet upon beadlet bombarded and beclouded the windscreen, only to be swept into oblivion by the wipers' metronomic energy.

Suddenly – but who knows if the thing hadn't insinuated itself into my ken a while back without my registering it? – a smudge of watery white light showed up through the murk of the glass like an unidentified blip on a radar screen.

It grew larger and larger.

[2]

Then, just as I realised what it must be, the accident occurred.

The road was bordered in the French style by twin rows of plane trees, their usually neat hairdos tousled by the torrential rain. Before I had time to figure out what was happening around me, a flash of lightning, a perfect upper-case *Z* in form, streaked down the sky. I watched it make a beeline for one of the planes on the verge of the road just ahead of me and instantly envelop its bark in a thin flame of *crêpe Suzette* blue. A vaudevillian puff of smoke arose from the tree's mossy base, followed by an intestinal creak and a deafening thunderclap from which the whole countryside seemed to shudder. Then the trunk haggardly dragged itself into the air by the roots and redescended on the sopping wet asphalt in a weird slow-motion swoon.

With a panicky dual impulse, holding the steering wheel at full arm's length, I pinned my head against the seat's leopard-skin coverlet and pressed down on the brakes. Ancient tyres yelping under my feet, I lurched into the windscreen only to be stalled, no more than inches from disfigurement, by a cruel jab in the pit of my stomach from the buckle of the seat-belt. The car came to a halt, a huge black mass barring its way. A solidified chunk of darkness had detached itself from the firmament and plummeted across the road.

I switched the wipers off; as I did so, the white blip just as abruptly disappeared. I stayed put for a minute or so wondering if my heart would ever quit pounding against the seat-belt. I craved the poisonous solace of nicotine, but even though a crash had been averted I continued to harbour the fear, irrational as it was, that the Mini might go up in smoke. I unclicked the belt, opened the car door and shakily got out. The air felt wondrously cool on my cheeks.

My eye was caught first by an unsightly jagged-tooth gap in the right-hand row of planes. The tree whose number had come up straddled the road, completely blocking it. Horizontal, prostrate, singled out as it had been by the force of destiny, it impressed me as much thicker in girth, solider and denser, than any of its fellows still left standing. This is a tree, I thought, this is what a tree really looks like.

I lit a cigarette which, although I struggled to shelter it from the rain, was at once as discoloured as a cornpaper Gauloise. I now knew where the blip had come from. There was another car, and another driver, stationed on the far side of the plane. But, my chest heaving, my heart humping, I was – as yet – incurious about either.

I finally heard a man's voice: 'Ah ça – ça, c'est commode!'
I could only think of replying, stupidly, 'Oui.'
There was a silence, then:
'You there. Are you English?'
'Yes . . . yes I am.'
It was a disagreeable sensation conversing with someone off-screen. Where was he? Why didn't he show himself?

His car, however, had swum into focus: a Rolls-Royce, silver most likely. For the precise hue to be ascertained, it would have had to be inspected in natural daylight, like a pair of new shoes tried on in a shop with fluorescent lighting.

[4]

No more than a few seconds later the driver emerged. There had been no underhand motivation behind his protracted invisibility. He had been standing on the left bank of the road, concealed from my view by the tangled, bunched-up leaves of the excruciatingly flared tree. He was tall and forty-fivish. In the semi-darkness I had the impression of his being, not plump, but completely without angles. He was wearing a beautifully cut blue or blue-grey pinstriped suit and had hurriedly slung a trenchcoat over his shoulders. His neck was rakishly framed by its turned-up collar.

He made a gesture of indefinable significance across the trunk.

'Jean-Marc Cheret. So sorry we cannot shake hands,' he said in stiltedly unaccented English.

'Guy Lantern.'

We approached the trunk together like tennis players walking towards the net at the conclusion of some sweaty bout.

Rainbursts blossomed on Cheret's trenchcoat. He seemed more irritable than unnerved. He perfunctorily kicked the trunk, out of sheer frustration rather than because he fancied he could ever shift it.

'Merde! Oh, merde merde merde merde merde!'

'It could have been worse, I suppose,' I said glibly.

'Worse?'

'It could have fallen on one of us.'

'Ah yes,' Cheret said. 'Yes indeed, it could have fallen on one of us. Or maybe on both of us. It could have knocked both of us out with one –' He sighed, beginning to find his sarcasm, as I did, seriously unhelpful. 'But since we were spared that fate, what are we to do? We cannot stay here all night. And, as you see, there is a ditch on either side of the road. We cannot go around.'

I considered the situation. 'Look,' I said, 'what about this? I suggest one of us wait by the roadside for any cars that might come along while the other makes a U-turn in search of a telephone or a garage.'

'Il n'en est pas question,' Cheret answered brusquely, as if he were speaking to himself. Then he said, in a more ingratiating tone of voice: 'Forgive me. Much as it pains me to admit it, this tree, the lightning – they undoubtedly saved our lives. I don't know about you, but I would have ploughed into your little car if I hadn't been stopped in time. Your suggestion, though – I am afraid it's out of the question. I have a ferry to catch, the last ferry from Cherbourg. It is imperative I catch it.'

'Well, I'm sorry, but I don't –'

He interrupted me.

'But wait, you give me an idea there. What are your plans?'

'I beg your pardon?'

'Your plans, your projects – I mean to say, where are you going now?'

I was bewildered by the question but couldn't think of any good reason not to answer it.

'To Saint-Malo.'

'Saint-Malo?'

'Yes. I'm on a sort of holiday.'

'Saint-Malo, that is ideal. And for how long, may I ask?'

'Five or six days. I have to be in England again by Monday week.'

'Excellent. I see we shall do a deal,' said Cheret.

'A deal? What sort of a deal?'

'Why, haven't you guessed, my dear fellow?' he continued chummily.

(*Had* I guessed? Perhaps I already had.)

'An exchange,' said a now almost jovial Cheret. 'We must swap cars.'

I giggled. 'You aren't serious?'

'Of course I am serious.' Cheret was purring as smoothly as the engine of his Rolls. 'It is the simplest, the neatest solution to our mutual difficulty. It is the *only* solution. Here . . .' Over the trunk he handed me a small white square card. On it, in embossed lettering, I read by the wan flutter of my cigarette lighter flame:

JEAN-MARC CHERET

SPECIALISTE EN BEAUX-ARTS

and in the lower right-hand corner:

Villa Lazarus
14 rue du Pavot
Saint-Malo
36125212

'I am, as you see, a specialist of the fine arts. I – now how can I best express this? – I have clients, whom I advise. Who pay me to advise them. Handsomely, I might add. One of these clients is in need of my services. Across the Channel. A Lebanese gentleman, rich and generous – an increasingly rare combination, I'm afraid – and fond of very lovely, very expensive *objets d'art*. I have just received from him an imperious call, the kind of call that, you know, "brooks no denial".' The quotation marks were doubtless unintentional, but audible all the same, as Cheret lovingly savoured the alien expression on his tongue. 'I will be in England for two or three days at most – the time to advise my client, renew some contacts in Cork Street, then back to Saint-Malo. If we were to exchange cars, don't you see, we could both make what you call a U-turn, complete our journeys and in three days' time meet up again at my home – you have the address on my card – to exchange them back. No problem, no hassle. After reporting what has happened to the authorities, we each of us go about our business. What do you say?'

Plausible Cheret. As plausible as if he were proposing to sell me the Rolls, not lend it to me. Even so.

'I won't, if you don't mind.'

'Well, why not, for heaven's sake?'

'It's not that I don't trust you, you understand, but I'd really prefer not to complicate an already awkward situation.'

Cheret tetchily bared his wristwatch to the rain.

'Look here, Lantern, time is passing. You speak of not trusting me.' He overruled my objection. 'I understand your

[*8*]

reluctance. But, when all is said and done, I am willing to trust you with my Rolls-Royce and all I ask in return is a few days' use of your, I suspect, second-hand . . .' The sentence trailed off in a rather galling fashion. 'I am comprehensively insured. Are you?'

'Naturally I am.'

'Where, then, is the complication? Besides,' he added, 'isn't this the way lifelong friendships are sealed?'

I stood for a moment, motionless. The rain was coming down in earnest. My hair was matted across my brow. My shirt collar was clammily contracting about the nape of my neck. My shoes were grudgingly but surely letting in. Only yards in front of me reposed the gleaming Rolls.

'Yes – agreed,' I heard myself say.

'Sound fellow,' said Cheret, once again consulting his watch. He then sped back to the Rolls, from which, in a trice, he removed a shiny black attaché case and an overnight bag.

'Now, don't forget, it's a left-hand drive,' he said when he had returned. 'You'll soon get used to it. Easier than yours in France. And we'll meet up Thursday at the villa. Or Friday, if you prefer. Take your time. Enjoy yourself.'

I hesitated still, as if the decision had not yet been taken. But the indecent swiftness with which Cheret was expediting his end of the deal left me no time for second thoughts. From the Mini I extricated my luggage, a battered suitcase and a couple of tennis racquets. Cheret meanwhile had taken a crisp white shirt out of his overnight bag. He unwrapped it, snapped off a branch of the plane tree and raised an impromptu flag in the rain.

'It will have to do. Don't forget, though – at the first telephone kiosk, ring in to tell the authorities.'

I nodded. Whereupon, with a reciprocal *bon voyage*, we exchanged car keys and climbed past each other over the tree. I nervously got in the Rolls, a far, far roomier job than my Mini, and settled myself into its stylish oak-brown interior. Through the dusky windscreen I glimpsed, tremulously poised on the bonnet, the silver-plated Spirit of Ecstasy. I grasped the steering wheel in both hands, let them run over it for a few seconds, then switched on the ignition.

A minute later, as if by remote control, our two cars, God's Dinky toys, made simultaneous U-turns and departed in opposite directions.

It was nearly nine o'clock in the evening when, having stopped *en route* to ring the authorities as instructed, having then gobbled up the same monotonously dark mute road, digested it and spewed it out behind me, I found myself at last in the outlying streets of Saint-Malo.

Saint-Malo, I have to say, struck me at first as being as grim and inhospitable a provincial French town as any other I had ever known. Old, shuttered-up houses alternated with modern blocks of council flats. A dim street corner was suddenly flooded with the frosty light of a self-service filling station, like that of an open refrigerator in an unlit kitchen. No pedestrians were out and about. The pretty Saint-Malo, the quaint Saint-Malo, the scenic Saint-Malo of the tourist guide I had tucked into my suitcase that very morning, was out there somewhere, but the streets I drove through were so anonymous and narrow that, for the first time since taking leave of Cheret, I felt self-conscious about the size and pomp of the Rolls-Royce. Twice, on even so unrelievedly cheerless a Sunday night, I was forced to back up to let another car pass, and I decided to pull in at whatever halfway respectable hotel came my way.

I didn't have too far to go. Rounding a corner, I at once saw, vertical against the sideways-slanting rain, the letters *H*, *O*, *T* and *E* – as I took them in, the missing *L* lit up, twitched convulsively once or twice as if it had a cinder in its eye and sputtered out again. I slowed down to get a closer look. It was a one-star establishment, its uninspiring façade nevertheless exhibiting the myriad lapel badges that even the most wretched hotels in France invariably manage to accumulate over the years. A drab foyer was lighted but there was no one to be seen in it. Behind the unsavoury lace curtains of a ground-floor window I could make out what looked to be a combined bar and television room. Just perceptible was the pale blue shimmer of an animate screen, but I noticed no one sitting in front of it.

Although I've never been particular when it comes to hotels, I would certainly have passed on this one, had it not been for the hour of the evening and the rain; had it not equally been for the fact, the clinching fact, that adjacent to the hotel proper was a small courtyard in which three cars had already been bedded down for the night. Concerned as I was about parking another man's car in the street, beginning as well to feel a faint pang of remorse that I had ever let myself fall in with Cheret's crackpot scheme, I made up my mind on the spot and turned off into the yard.

The hotel was named, comically, L'Hôtel de l'Apothéose. I waited for a moment at the unoccupied reception desk. Beneath its transparent glass overlay, which felt as slick and brittle to my damp fingers as the glazing on a *crème brûlée*, there had been spread out flat a map of the region, annotated with belching East and West Winds and diminutive golfers, yachtsmen and water-skiers. On the wall opposite me was a square rack of hollow compartments, four by four, each of which contained, or else not, a key to one of the rooms. (Only two out of the sixteen keys were missing.) Next to that hung a reproduction of a Dufy seascape and a list of dubiously reasonable rates. On the desk itself, beside an outmoded black telephone, as heavy and bland as a mugger's blunt instrument, was a rolled-up copy of *L'Equipe*. There was also a tiny bell, which, after some further vacillation, I rang. To my surprise, when I did, a night clerk immediately popped up from behind the desk, where he had been stretched out on a sofa.

He was an elderly man, of Corsican appearance, with a proletarian swarthiness that hadn't been acquired in Saint-Malo. He blinked once or twice, as if, seeing me there, he could scarcely believe his dozy eyes. Then he said, in a thick Marseillais accent:

'Monsieur?'

I asked for a room with a bath or shower.

'Ce sont toutes des chambres avec salle de bain,' he replied.

He turned to the rack, unhooked the very first key and handed it over to me.

'C'est au premier. Bonne nuit, monsieur.'

That appeared to be all there was to it.

I was a little dumbfounded. I had never before had Room No. 1 in a hotel. It was one of those things you just never expected to happen to you, like being the very first passenger to board a plane. I looked blankly at the key for a few seconds, the night clerk's smile humouring me all the while. Finally, I enquired whether there weren't any formalities to be undergone, something to fill in, maybe. Didn't he even want to know my name?

The clerk shook his head.

'Le matin, monsieur. Vous ferez tout ça le matin. Ne vous inquiétez-vous pas, monsieur.'

Would it be possible, I then asked him, to have some food sent up to my room? – but I knew, as soon as I had voiced it, what a foolish request *that* was.

Sadly shaking his head as if he were of the same opinion, the clerk picked up the rolled copy of *L'Equipe*.

'Mais non, vous voyez bien, y a pas de tel service ici. Bonne nuit, monsieur.'

I turned my eyes in the direction of the glass doorway at the end of the hall. It was still raining. A blustery wind, too, had blown up: within the doorway's oblong frame three passing sailors staggered like drunken pierrots. Then a raincoated man stamped past the hotel holding, like a battering ram, a large striped umbrella at a direct right angle to himself. As I watched, it blew inside out and he was propelled forward out of sight. With a sigh, I picked up my suitcase – I didn't even ask about the possibility of having the clerk carry it up for me – and ascended the dark staircase to my room, which, modest, clean and serviceable, turned out to be identical to every small hotel room in the world.

I went to bed at half-past-ten, after unpacking and showering. More from force of habit than because I thought the night would be a noisy one, I opened a little box of earplugs, pink wax *boules Quiès*, and stopped my ears with the last two unused ones.

They were still as fluffy as when I had bought them and, underneath the fluff, as rosy as marzipan. I don't remember falling asleep.

I awoke at eight-thirty and might have slept even longer had I not been gently stirred out of unconsciousness by the inquisitive light flowing through the window blind I had forgotten to pull down the evening before. It had not been a good night. I had dreamed the same dream that I always did, the dream that wasn't a dream, that was, instead, a terrifyingly limpid reproduction – accurate to the last detail, so far as I could any longer tell – of an instant which, when it had actually taken place, had felt paradoxically dreamlike: the howl of tyres, the Gothic arch of snow-drenched trees above our heads, the lone snowman in the field, fainting in the sun like a guardsman on parade, Ursula's face at the point of impact, her face on which I turned helplessly to gaze . . .

I flung the first-floor window open and stuck my head out. The day was dry and fresh. The sky was white. It was no longer raining and the wind had blown itself away. Its sails deflated, Saint-Malo was slowly drifting out to sea.

I padded into the bathroom to shave. It was past nine o'clock and I had missed the chance of ordering breakfast in my room. ('Le petit déjeuner complet est servi dans les chambres entre 7.30 et 09.00,' I was informed by a sign pinned to the door. 'Le petit déjeuner anglais: supplément de 45 francs.') I would have a coffee and croissant in town.

Downstairs, in the foyer, a proud little Scottish family of tartan suitcases, father, mother and two twin offspring half their size, stood primly lined up against the reception desk, but there still wasn't a soul around, neither arriving nor departing guests, no one save the same clerk I had spoken to the evening before.

Like the weather he too had changed. He had shaved the clouds off his face for one thing and rinsed the forking ditches of grime out of its wrinkles. Beaming at me as I stepped forward to the desk, he greeted me in English.

'Good morning, monsieur. You slept well, I hope?'

'Very well, thank you,' I replied, slipping the key across to him. 'May I sign in now, please?'

'Unfortunately, monsieur, the *patronne* is not in yet. But it is not a problem, you know. When you come back this afternoon, okay?'

'As you prefer,' I said calmly, mystified though I was by his continuing indifference to officialising my residence in the hotel. Then, tapping the two inside breast pockets of my jacket to make sure that one of them contained my wallet, the other my passport, I prepared to leave.

'It is *yours*, is it not?' the clerk unexpectedly said to me.

'Mine?'

'The automobile.'

'The . . . Oh, I see, you mean the . . .' I glanced in the direction of the car park outside. 'Mmm . . .' Then I heard myself unblushingly say, 'Well, yes, it *is* mine – for my sins.'

He shook a rubbery right hand in the French prole's traditional gesture of envy and admiration.

'Belle bagnole! Une Rolls-Royce, n'est-ce pas? Ou plutôt, comme vous l'appelez tous, vous autres Anglais, une "Rolls".'

'A Royce, actually.'

'Une quoi?'

'A Royce. Une "Royce", pas une "Rolls".'

He stared at me in gratifying bafflement.

'Not that it's of any consequence, you understand,' I said with a simper, and heaven knows where I dredged up this piece of trivia – or why, for that matter – 'but those of us who own one call it a Royce.'

'Une Royce, dites-vous? Première nouvelle, monsieur.'

'As I say, you have to own one to know.'

I nodded good day to him and sashayed jauntily into the street.

Cleansed by the night's rainfall, the Rolls glittered in the morning air. It was, as I had surmised, silver; and now that I saw it in daylight for the first time, I confess I was bowled over by what a magnificent car it was, irrefutably the best in the world. I watched how passers-by – of whom there were few enough, for the Hôtel de l'Apothéose appeared to be situated in a rather backwatery *quartier* – would turn their heads leftward or rightward, as if taking a military salute, to stare at it as they passed. I had never really understood before how radically a material possession could amend one's self-image.

Somewhere, far away, a gull screamed. It so happened there was a café, not overly lively-looking, at the end of the street on which I was dithering, and I decided to breakfast there. I chose a table deep in its fuggy interior and ordered a hot chocolate and a croissant. Over my shoulder I could hear the oddly satisfying click of marble spheres, buffeted from obstacle to obstacle, rolling down the inclined plane of a pinball machine. I began to read from my visitor's guide to Saint-Malo.

On the northwest side of the France's hexagon, a half way between Cape Fréhel and the Grouin headland, the bay of Saint-Malo forms part of that Channel coastline which, since the start of the century, has been called the Emerald Coast and which, between Erquy and Granville, also composes the bay of Mont Saint-Michel. From east to west, this coast offers thus some particularly various paysages. To the east, from Cancale to the mouthpiece of the Sélune, are the vast flat expanses of the Mont Saint-Michel bay, with its polders reclaimed from the sea and its sand strands, from which the tide is known to withdraw at certain points more than ten kilometres from the coastline.

I looked at the contents page of the guide, which I had purchased at Blackwell's in Oxford. There was no author's name inscribed on it nor any indication that the text might be a translation from the French – which in one sense, to be sure, it wasn't. I skimmed the next few paragraphs.

The ramparts itself forms the classic Saint-Malo walk, the one that every self-respecting inhabitant (or Malouin) is forced to carry out at least once a day! Without hurrying, one can thus in less than an hour achieve the tour of the whole town, which is, by the way, not a large town, its perimeter being not excessive of one nautical mile (1,852 metres). By circling Saint-Malo in this style, one can better appreciate both the site and the architecture. The ramparts form a tall balcony above the beaches and the bay where one can follow, especially in the high season, the evolution of the sailing races and the windsurfings.

Whether it was because or in spite of so garbled an endorsement I could hardly have said, but I thought, why not? I would inaugurate my holiday in Saint-Malo with the famous classic walk.

Paying my bill at the café, navigating my route by the indelible aroma of the Atlantic, I walked through the silent streets of that part of town in which I had spent the night, streets in which nondescript and not even particularly lofty office blocks had sprung up, no doubt since the Allied bombardment, like weeds in a herbaceous border. I entered the old walled quarter by what continued to be called its New Gate – it had been erected, so alleged a sign, in 1709 – and passed under a vaulted arcade bearing Saint-Malo's coat-of-arms and the motto *Semper Fidelis*. I turned into a cobblestoned passage, its dungeon-like door opening on to a shadowy recess in which, my travel guide instructed me, all seventeenth-century travellers attempting to enter the town after the ten o'clock curfew would have been held overnight. Then, at last, I mounted the ramparts, which snaked about the coastline like the Great Wall of China.

The sky was flecked with slim blue streamers trailing what I hoped were days of uninterrupted cloudlessness to come, and the ramparts were already crammed with promenading couples training their cameras on the oyster-toned ocean and the gull-encircled National Fort and the rocky pedestrian causeway that led out to it and that had been left high and dry by the low tide to become as muddy underfoot as suburban linoleum on a drizzly afternoon. There were scores of such couples, young, middle-aged, elderly – these tended to be the English ones – wearing plastic mackintoshes that blazed in the pale sunlight. There were families, too, of every nationality, their children joyfully racing on ahead until seized with the fear that they might unwittingly have ventured outside their parents' orbit: I took a perverse pleasure in watching these children stop dead in their little tracks and crane uneasily about the hulking bodies of strangers until gladly relocating a set of recognisable features amid a sea of uncaptioned faces. And there were groups, coach parties of Germans and Swiss and Japanese – even a ubiquitous party of black Africans whom I could never quite shake off. Surrounded by them, as I chanced to be at one stage on the *chemin de ronde*, surrounded by their manly black faces and dazzling white teeth, I felt like the one unappetisingly white chocolate that gets left to last in a box filled with otherwise conventionally dark ones.

And it was then, all at once, that the fatal question which had been hovering over me from the moment I'd left the hotel – from the moment, who knows, I'd left England – alit at long last and forced me to face it. *What, oh God, what am I doing here?* I looked bleakly about me. There was no escaping it: myself apart, no one was by himself. Or herself. No one. Alone, I was doubly alone: I was also alone in being alone. I was that most dispiriting of human types, a type to whom the great, vibrant constituency of the living gives a wider berth than to any outright scoundrel: a 'sad' man, someone of whom it is suspected that 'he doesn't have much of a life'. It was then, I say, and childishly nonsensical as it may seem to someone who has never found himself in such a situation, for it happened no more than an hour after I had set off so gaily from the Apothéose, that I knew I couldn't go on, I simply couldn't go on.

What a grotesque idea it had been to spend a week on my own at Saint-Malo. At Saint-Malo! Why dreary old Saint-Malo, in heaven's name? Why not Boulogne, like a loutish day tripper stocking up on cheap red wine? Why not Dieppe, like Robbie Ross and Reggie Turner at the turn of the century, imagining, because they had braved the Channel, that they were 'travelling'. Why not Ostend, like some spinster from Cheltenham blowing her inheritance − but even spinsters travelled in twos!

Saint-Malo? Who gives a damn, who gives a shit, who gives a tinker's curse, for its ramparts, for its *harmonious and symmetrical engineer's architecture'*, as my guidebook typically put it, for its ludicrously named Hôtel White where Chateaubriand lived in his childhood? Who gives a damn for Chateaubriand or his childhood? No one, not really, not truthfully, not secretly − not one of these couples, these families, these groups, whose pointlessly zigzagging paths I was crossing, all of whom were feeling, I knew, *I knew*, just as waywardly adrift as I was but all of whom had at least each other to feel adrift with. Some of them I would even catch, literally, furtively, glancing at their wristwatches as if wondering when they could decently pack up and go home, where life had a point and a direction, even if it wasn't always easy to say what it was. There was no point here, there was no direction save that of the famous classic walk, which none of us dared transgress.

What a farce! Whatever could I have been thinking of? How beside every imaginable point come to seem all the promise and planning that we put into travel – into even a wretched week in Saint-Malo – when we are at last confronted with the real thing. Are we fated never to fathom ourselves, never to take ourselves in our stride?

No, no, I couldn't go on. The insipid beauties of the picturesque fell on my shoulders like a dead weight. I felt my own watch clinging tenaciously to my wrist and sucking time out of it like a leech. I felt conspicuous, conspicuously solitary. I felt as if, were I to remain a day longer, even an hour longer, in this godforsaken town, I would end up making wretched small talk to some sweet old English couple minding their own business as they walked about the *chemin de ronde* or even – what a hideous, what a humiliating thought! – to some other pathetic loner like myself, always assuming I could find one.

My head was buzzing, and I feared I was about to have the kind of brief but intense seizure that had been, for the past several months, among the scarier side-effects of my medication. To my left, beyond the forest of humanity swaying ahead of me, I spied a steep stone staircase leading back down into the old town and made for it as rapidly as I could. I descended it three steps at a time, nearly losing my footing in my fretful eagerness to be off the ramparts. It was quiet down there, free of pedestrians. With a trembling hand I lit a cigarette and for a while just stood and inhaled its deliciously toxic fumes.

Most unusually for me, I had a second helping, and a third. By one o'clock, after that third cigarette, I felt tranquillised, my soul appeased. I was ready to take action. Past pastry shops, and kiosks selling postcards and souvenirs, and cafés serving nothing but Breton *galettes* and *crêpes*, along cramped, winding streets made nearly impassible by the crowds, I slowly walked back to the Hôtel de l'Apothéose. I was taking my time because I needed to collect my thoughts.

The trip had been a ghastly mistake, that I knew – even the hotel's night clerk seemed to have understood that I wouldn't be around long enough to make it worth his while regularising my presence. And I was already beginning to wonder whether I might return to England that very day, simply refuse to throw good time after bad and catch the first ferry back, so that no one would ever know of my folly but myself, when, nearing the hotel, I caught sight of Cheret's car parked in the car park. The Rolls! The fucking Royce! With a sensation close to terror I realised that I was stranded in Brittany for three days at least. I could not leave – not until Cheret returned with my Mini. My eyes welled with tears. Damn him! Damn his ingenious solution to our mutual problem!

I also realised that I was ravenously hungry. I unlocked the car door, edged myself into the driver's seat and flicked through my guidebook. Since I could not face eating alone in a proper restaurant, the one I eventually plumped for wasn't listed among the guide's own recommendations but was advertised in the margin of one of its pages. The advertisement depicted a deliriously sporty couple of indeterminate age eyeing with rapture a monstrous pudding trolley which had just been wheeled up to their table by a radiant *maître d'hôtel* in a tuxedo. In truth, it was its very imbecility that appealed to me, for I now knew how fatuous had been the epicurean fantasies I had entertained before setting out from England – of a succession of three-star meals consumed in solitary bliss. La Belle France! What a farce, what a farce!

My ambition having been reduced to this, merely to relieve my hunger, I launched the Rolls-Royce out of the hotel's car park and on to the street as ceremoniously as if it were an aircraft carrier. For, oh, as I now discovered, what a blastedly cumbersome contraption it was! It would advance with all the pachydermic dignity and deliberation of a maharajah's elephant, forcing idle groups of tourists, who had been ambling along the middle of the road, to make a jittery rush for left or right. For the first time I felt definite twinges of nostalgia for my dear, unbossy, uncomplaining Mini.

As the minutes passed, too, I felt something else. I had an increasingly distinct hunch that I was being watched. To begin with, I imagined that someone was trailing me, another car following mine, and I kept a craning eye on the rear-view mirror. Yet, even though I soon felt reassured that no one automobile had remained within the mirror's frame since I left the Apothéose, I still couldn't rid myself of the sensation that my progress through the town was under some sort of unseen surveillance, and I stretched my neck, when passing below the ramparts, to check whether one of the telescopes spaced out along them, telescopes in which you inserted a ten-franc coin if you had an urge to examine the horizon in close-up, had been swung about on its axis and directed down on to the streets of Saint-Malo itself – down on to me. But it was hopeless. Notwithstanding the snail's crawl at which I moved through the old town's impenetrable thoroughfares, I was never able to slow down long enough.

Then, at an intersection, just as the traffic lights had turned red against me, my eye was irresistibly drawn to a man crossing the road who all of a sudden turned his head in my direction, for no purpose that I could discern, and gazed into my windscreen. In truth, when I'd first noticed him, he was still standing at the kerbside, his chubby fingers interlinked across his embonpoint like the buckle of a schoolboy's snake-clasp belt; and, if he caught my eye, it was because, obese and blubbery, he couldn't have been less like the slim, dapper little fellow, now red and cautious, now green and go-ahead, lit up on the panel of the traffic lights just above his head. He intrigued me, too, by being both overdressed and under-dressed: overdressed in that he had on a staidly cut suit of the 'bespoke' Savile Row sort, a suit that seemed very out of place in a Breton seaside resort; yet underdressed as well, in that he wasn't wearing any coat over that suit, and this on a day on which the sun was still far from coming to the boil. About a quarter of the way across the street, he turned to face me. An almost imperceptible shadow of anxiety rippled over his jowly features. He stopped dead in his tracks for a split second – or was it only in my imagination? – then passed on and the lights turned to green in my favour . . .

The brasserie I had chosen was exactly what I had expected it to be, a luminous glass cage, its noise and agitation blasting out at me, when I passed through its revolving door, as if I had just turned up the volume on a radio. Outside, a huddle of shivering lunchers were seated together on a canopied terrace, shielding their *croque-monsieurs* against the wind. Inside, it was warm and clammy. I paused on the threshold, thought to turn back and try my luck elsewhere. But where?

No one came forward to greet me, no one hankered after my custom. I might have been invisible for all anyone cared. I stood there, at a loss, while waiters circulated with trays of *choucroute*, obviously a house speciality, and crustaceans nestling on black seaweed, and thermidor lobsters as splendid as crown jewels in their glamorous red carapaces. I tried as best I could to respect everyone's space, but wherever I parked myself I seemed to be in the way of someone or other. It was as if my presence alone, my very aloneness, had the effect of a subtle sedative, a mild depressant, on those who had the misfortune to be lunching in my vicinity. I could actually hear their conversation losing its snap and sparkle at my approach. And still no one came to seat me.

I finally approached the head waiter and asked outright for a table.

He looked me up and down.

'Vous êtes seul, monsieur?'

'Oui, je suis,' I said maladroitly.

He at once switched to English.

'I am sorry, monsieur,' he said, shrugging the whole upper half of his body in a parodically French fashion, 'but if you are alone you will not mind to share a table.'

He briskly escorted me towards a *banquette* for two, at which already sat a middle-aged man with a plate of *moules marinières* in front of him. Wearing a charcoal-grey tie, a dark V-necked pullover under a navy-blue suit, on whose lapel was affixed a minute red rosette, and a pair of rimless glasses, he assuredly wasn't a tourist. He looked up at me as I removed my coat, acknowledged my arrival with the ghost of a smile and unhurriedly shifted a motoring magazine, still in its subscriber's wrapper, from my half of the table. The head waiter handed me a menu as large as a tabloid newspaper and, without giving it too much attention, I ordered a bowl of onion soup, a grilled sole and a carafe of white wine.

Not long after I'd started eating the soup, the man at my side addressed me.

'You see that car?' he asked me in French.

'Pardon?'

'I said, do you see that car?'

'What car?'

'There. In the car park.'

I turned round. Framed in the nearest window, dwarfing all the cars beside it, was the Rolls-Royce. Its radiator had captured what scant sunlight there was about and it grinned at us in toothy self-confidence. No question, it was a masterpiece.

I turned once more to face my table-mate.

'Can you imagine getting behind the steering wheel of that?' he sighed, wiping with his napkin a moustache that was sepia with nicotine stains. 'If I knew when I got up in the morning that I'd be driving to work in that beauty, I wouldn't have to be wakened twice, I can tell you.'

'It's mine,' I said, raising a spoonful of soup to my lips.

'What?'

'It's mine. It's my car.'

Behind his glasses, which were now perched midway along the bridge of his nose like a spare pair of eyes, he fixed his sights on me for a second or two without speaking. Then, with a phlegmy if-you-say-so clearing of the throat, he returned to his *moules*, draining first the meat then the juice out of each of them in turn before depositing, on a pile that had been steadily rising on his side plate, an empty shell as black as a crow's beak.

It wasn't until I had finished my soup and was waiting for my sole to be served that he spoke again.

'Eh, dites-moi, mon ami,' he said, and the skin of his face was raw from the steam that had been pouring off his plate.

'Yes?'

'That Rolls-Royce? It's yours, you say?'

'Yes,' I replied, slightly irritated by the undertow of mockery I detected in his voice, 'I believe that is what I said.'

'Then why, please,' he began – and even before I knew

what he was going to say I wanted to slap his big red splotchy moon face – 'why is somebody else driving it away?'

If I had been sipping wine at that instant, I would have choked on it like a gauche young lead in a screwball comedy. Instead, I looked back out of the window. There could be no doubt of it at all. The Rolls was gliding away from the car park.

To my companion's slack-jawed stupefaction, I leapt to my feet, grabbed my overcoat from the chair-back, knocking the chair itself to the floor as I did so. I elbowed past customers about to take their seats or about to vacate them and rampaged across the room to the door. I shoved it open, neither knowing nor frankly caring whether I risked bloodying someone's nose in the process, and was just in time to see the Rolls-Royce, its driver as yet a mysteriously unknown quantity, gingerly making its way down the street. Flabbergasted, I started to chase after it and at the same time, forgetting my French in the heat of the crisis, shouted out, ridiculously yet inevitably, 'Help! Help! Stop thief! Stop thief!'

As I shouted, I heard someone else shout behind me, in French, 'Au voleur!'

Au voleur! Of course. How could I have forgotten so elementary an expression?

Englishman that I ineradicably was, I turned to thank whoever it was who had offered me so providential a prompt, so unlooked-for a translation, and I saw the restaurant's head waiter, short of breath and puce of complexion, standing beside me.

'Je vous remercie bien, monsieur,' I said warmly.

He laid his hands on my shoulder.

'Ah ça – ça – ça, c'est quelque chose!' he spat in my face. 'Vous êtes drôle, vous! Vous – vous criez "au voleur" quand c'est vous-même, le voleur!'

I stared at him.

'Me? A thief? What in Christ's name are you talking about? It's *my* car that's been stolen.'

Without easing his grip on my shoulder, he held up a piece of white paper to my face, as close as if about to rub my nose in it. It turned out to be the bill for my lunch, the lunch I'd eaten part of but, as it only then occurred to me, not paid for at all. There was no time for an argument. Although it was hard to credit that anyone could be as obtuse as this moron of a head waiter, as obnoxiously inconsiderate under what were patently exceptional circumstances, and although I found myself recalling every ugly anti-French stereotype I had heard over the years and had always faithfully pooh-poohed, I drew out my wallet, thrust a two-hundred-franc note at him and set off in pursuit of Cheret's receding Rolls-Royce.

Saint-Malo's streets had been laid out with horses, not automobiles, in mind, so that the thief must have had the same problems manoeuvring the Rolls through them as I myself had had that morning. Yet although I ran after it faster than I'd run in several years, and constantly had to swerve this way and that to avoid the throng of tourists, it seemed always to be the case that whenever I turned a corner all I would see was the car itself turning the corner at the other end of the same street and once more vanishing from my sight. I would turn and it would turn. I would turn and it would turn. It happened time and time again, so systematically I started to wonder whether there wasn't some sort of curse upon me. For fear, too, of making myself look even sillier than I already felt, I could no longer bring myself to cry for help, in either English or French. I simply could not, would not, pronounce the words 'Stop thief!' or 'Au voleur!' Nor, all the while I ran, did I see a single policeman.

In the end I lost sight of the Rolls altogether and took a few minutes out to lean, despondent, against the garden wall of a bungalow. Attempting to calm an atrocious stitch in my chest, one that made me clutch at my heart like a tenor, I peered about me. I was in what appeared to be an exclusively residential *quartier*, shady, calm and bourgeois. There was, on the wall of every single house in the street, a sleek black marble plaque into which had been carved – in a bold convolvular script, a script that mimicked, like a lizard, the fern and ivy that threatened precisely to blot it out – some whimsical appellation, the French equivalent, I supposed, of 'Dunroamin' or even 'Chez Nous'. As a street to live in, it might, I suppose, have been considered by many a trifle prosy and middle-class. At the same time, there was a vaguely sinister edge to it, as if anything were possible, anything could happen, behind such immaculate façades, such fine muslin curtains, such meticulously clipped cockerels and giraffes.

A butterfly – that could have escaped from my insides – waltzed in the unruffled air. Smidgens of sweat freckled my shirt-front. There wasn't a sign of the Rolls-Royce. I had no option left to me now but to retrace my steps to the town centre and report the theft. My only hope lay in the Rolls's size and uniqueness, which would surely make its concealment awkward, but I had next to no faith in the Saint-Malo constabulary. In any case, my holiday was over, wrecked, a calamity. And since I couldn't leave town until Cheret had returned, I wasn't even going to be allowed to call it a day there and then.

I started to walk back, to shamble back, to the hotel. And then, turning into the very next street, pretty much a duplicate of the one I had just left, I saw it. There, in the driveway of a 1920-ish villa – a villa whose low, white, horizontal roof lent it a hint of the Bauhaus – there, parked beside another, more modestly proportioned car, was the Rolls-Royce, having rematerialised out of thin air as miraculously as it had disappeared, simply to tease me.

The sight of it brought me a second wind and I dashed across the street. As I reached the driveway, a man, an outlandishly tall man, ageless, gaunt of form and feature, dressed in a coal-black, unbuttoned, double-breasted suit, reared up from behind the Rolls and made a lunge towards me. I strove to say something – to say what, I don't know, because not a word emerged. Too maddened to speak coherently, I tried to open the door on the driver's side. It was locked. I set about scrabbling in the pockets of my overcoat for the keys but was immediately pinned against the car. My assailant's hands were everywhere at once. One hand was outlined against the sky, another blocked out the villa's french window, a third, or what seemed like a third, struggled to unlock its front door. I squirmed, I screamed, I yanked at one of his lapels and succeeded only in ripping my thumb on something needle-like. I groaned and relaxed the feeble pressure I was exerting on him. Seizing his advantage, he clamped a knuckly hand over my lips and with the other took me by the scruff of my neck and lugged me – I wriggled like a schoolboy caught scrumping apples – up into the house, whose door was now open.

We were in a dark hallway. I tore at him, trying to scrape the palm of his hand off my mouth. He dragged me on. Some object clanged in the *demi-jour*. Without warning, I found myself in a spacious, high-ceilinged room flooded by sunlight.

We continued to scuffle. We slithered over polished parquet flooring until I snagged my foot on the edge of a rug and felt myself toppling over – I had a whirlingly confused view of a motif of blue-and-coral lozenges. As I fell, both my legs folding under me like a card table's, I saw, as if someone had screwily strung them up across the ceiling, a spinning succession of wall paintings, mostly period, eighteenth-century, as I somehow succeeded in making out, but there was also a Miró, unmistakable even to eyes as dazed as mine, and a large-scale portrait of a naked adolescent girl sprawling languorously in front of an open fireplace.

Then, behind me, I heard a woman's voice:

'Mais qu'est-ce que c'est que ce cinéma?'

The effect was instantaneous. My aggressor slackened his hold. With a sudden sullen regard for the proprieties, he removed his hand from my neck, even attempted to assist me to my feet. I wrenched myself free of him, quickly patted my hair down and turned to face whoever had spoken.

She was standing halfway up the staircase. She was in her late twenties or very early thirties, wearing a loose cream silk shirt and a pair of equally loose-fitting grey slacks, slacks whose subtly spoked pleats emphasised her small, neat waist. Her hair, blonde, drawn back tight from her forehead, fell heavy and straight on her shoulders; and her eyebrows, which were noticeably darker than her hair, had the form of two little, matchingly praying angels. Between the fingers of her right hand, which was posed on the staircase rail, she was holding a cigarette, and I saw, on her forefinger, a dull gold Roman ring of uneven measure, with no stone set in it.

She was tanned. Yet, from even as far away as I was standing, I could tell that it was the tan of money, not of the sun, the tan of poise and property, ease and security, a tan as natural to her race as ebony pigmentation is to a Zulu. Hers was the innately tanned skin, as if bronzed from the inside out, of those born to die rich.

But she had asked what the row was about and, half in

English, half in French, I explained that I had discovered my car, my stolen car, parked in the driveway of what I assumed was her house.

Without saying a word, she interrupted me. She walked to the foot of the staircase, crushed out her barely smoked cigarette, brutally buckling the fragile tube until it was as mangled as an old bicycle wheel in a junkyard, went to the window and looked out. She turned to face me, unsmiling.

'*Your* car, monsieur?'

'Well, no . . .'

'Hmm?'

'It's not precisely my car.'

'No. To be precise, it's my husband's.'

'Your husband's?' I stared at her. Then I stared about me. Of course, of course. Why hadn't I thought of it before? 'Now I understand. You must be Madame Cheret.'

'And you, monsieur? Who are you? And how do you come to be driving my husband's car?'

As concisely as I could, I related everything that had happened to me from my arrival in France the day before. I studied her face as I spoke. That she was astounded by my peculiar little narrative couldn't be doubted, and I interpreted such a reaction as the surest sign that she accepted it as the truth.

I hadn't been paying much attention to the man with whom I had scuffled in the driveway. But when I'd completed my story, Madame Cheret first, distractedly, nodded two or three times, as if my telling of it had been a necessary but finally tiresome formality, as if there had been nothing at all out of the ordinary in my adventure, as if to say, 'Yes, yes, of course, that's obviously what must have happened, why bother me with details?' Then she turned in his direction and with a wave of a newly lit cigarette murmured, 'Qu'est-ce que tu attends, mon ami? Va chercher la clé.'

At these words he strode towards the door. Although I found it queer that apologies were still to be given and accepted on both our behalves, I took it upon myself to point out that there was no need to fetch the car keys since I had them in my pocket. Still distracted, she again waved the other man off. Then she pulled herself out of whatever state she was in and we introduced ourselves. Her name was Béatrice.

'Naturally,' she said, 'you must keep the car for just as long as you and Jean-Marc agreed that you would.'

I made a meaningless sort of noise with, to my disgust, so many *n*'s in it that it sounded as if I were courteously declining her magnanimous offer (but, as I told myself, there could be no question of my not keeping the car), and actually heard myself apologising for the ruckus in her drawing room.

'Please,' she said. 'Please, it's I who should apologise. Sacha is devoted to my husband. When he saw the car in town, he must have imagined that something had happened to Jean-Marc, you understand . . .' Her voice trailed off, and for a few seconds she looked as distracted as before. Then she arched her wrist in front of her eyes as if to consult a watch.

There was none. She continued to gaze at her bare, tanned wrist. There was a wristwatch-shaped patch of pallor on it. 'I'm so sunburnt,' she said absently, 'I can almost tell the time without my watch.'

'It's a quarter-to-two,' I said, consulting my own.

'My poor friend, you must be starved.'

I accepted her invitation to stay for lunch.

We had lunch – cold cuts, omelette, salad and white Burgundy – in the dining room, just the three of us at one end of a long mahogany table: Béa, as she insisted I call her; my assailant, whose name was Sacha, Sacha Liebermann, and who, it transpired, was Jean-Marc's business partner; and myself. On the wall at the far end of the table, partially concealed by a setting of white roses, was a framed Chardin still life of a loaf of brown bread as crusty and sacramental as a human brain. Propped against a chair was another painting, a Braque, of a dove, as if abandoned there for want of anywhere better to put it, as if, on entering the villa, someone had just slung it on to the chair like a hat. The walls themselves had lately been stripped down and repainted in light, pastelly shades, and a spindly, six-candle iron chandelier hung low over our heads like a mammoth spider dangling from its web.

Picking at the food and the conversation alike, filling and refilling his glass, glaring at me balefully across the white roses, Sacha said little, ate little, and drank like a fish. Béa, on the other hand, could not have been more attentive; she even, unless I misread the signs, started flirting with me. When she pumped me on my background, I replied, telling only as much of the truth as I felt I could, that I was a writer – oh, just biographies, other people's biographies – 'that, I suppose,' I said with a rueful smile, 'is the story of my life' – and that I'd had a bout of illness – nothing too serious, a flu I couldn't get clear of, a suspicion of pneumonia that turned out to be a false alarm – and had decided to take a few days' break before returning to my work.

'And how are you enjoying your break?' she enquired vaguely.

I felt I'd had a trick question put to me. I hardly knew how to answer – I who, only an hour before, had been cursing my encounter with her husband and the aftermath to that encounter that now left me beached in Saint-Malo. For a moment I hummed and hawed, was gearing up definitively to haw, to reply with some politely turned negative, when the telephone rang.

She stood up to take the call, saying as she did so that it was probably Jean-Marc ringing to clear up the situation from his end. I found myself alone at table with Sacha. Chopping his lettuce into ever more minute particles, he was visibly under some sort of strain.

'Béa is charming,' I said, anxious to make conversation.

At this he bared whitish gums and startlingly discoloured teeth, but said nothing.

'She tells me you work with Jean-Marc,' I persisted. 'What does your work involve exactly?'

He didn't answer at first. Then he said, as unenthusiastically as if the words had to be prised out of him, 'This and that. Deals.'

'Oh yes?'

There was a pause, after which I added, 'I think you ought to know that in English' – we were speaking in English – 'when somebody says he does this and that for a living, it tends to sound, well, shady.'

'Shady? What is that?'

'You know, sort of illegal.'

Sacha stared at me, as well he might have, for only too late did it occur to me how impertinent my comment had been. I instantly clammed up and, at first unconsciously, then more attentively, tuned in to Béa's telephone conversation, disconnected snatches of which had already been floating back to us – the phone sat on top of a marble table in the corridor leading out of the dining room and Béa was half standing against it, half sitting on it, swinging a leg in front of her and examining its shoe's toecap.

'. . . Oui, oui, oui, c'est ça . . .' I heard her say. 'Mais tout à fait . . . puisque je vous le dis . . . oui, oui, ici-même . . . mais si, mais si, lui aussi est là . . . parfaitement . . . oui . . . d'ailleurs je le trouve plutôt séduisant . . . bien sûr . . . oui . . . oui . . . ne vous inquiétez pas . . . oh non, non, surtout pas ça . . . non . . . je trouverai un moyen . . . oui . . . oui . . . oui . . . au revoir.'

She rejoined us at table. Without making an allusion to the call, she immediately addressed me.

'What sounds illegal, Guy?'

It was Sacha who replied. His speech was slurred and Béa watched him closely as he spoke.

'My life. What I do. He thinks it must be illegal.'

I protested. 'No, really, you're misquoting me. I was simply pointing out that in English the word "deal" has a pejorative . . .'

'Deal?' said Béa, looking at both of us in turn, as if feeling excluded from some cryptic little game that Sacha and I were playing together. 'What deal are you talking about?'

'I asked Sacha what he did for a living and he said deals.'

Spreading a sliver of *pâté de fois gras* over a cracker, Béa distended her lips to expose a tiara of perfect white teeth.

'Well, I trust, once he makes one, he sticks to it.'

To which Sacha replied, 'Sometimes you have to renegotiate.'

'It takes two to renegotiate a deal,' said Béa.

'Two,' said Sacha, 'and sometimes three.'

'In my experience of business deals – if business *is* what we're talking about – three's a committee. Nothing ever gets done.'

'Funny,' said Sacha. 'What I heard was three's a crowd.'

This was too much for Béa. Angrily tossing her knife down on the table, she spoke in French again.

'Ne te rends pas ridicule, mon cher. Devant notre invité.'

'*Notre* invité? C'est gentil, ça. Eh bien, non.'

'Quoi?'

'Non, je te dis, non.'

'Mais quoi, non?'

'N'oublie pas qu'elle est à moi, la clé.'

'Tais-toi, imbécile.'

To which Sacha replied with a dry, cindery cackle, 'Comme disent nos amis anglais, "you can't argue with genius".'

Such was the contempt that could be read on Béa's face, I felt almost sorry for him.

'Cretin!' she snapped. 'I'm not arguing with genius. I'm arguing with you.'

Sacha appeared about to answer her, but had second thoughts. For my own part, I at once stood up, mumbling my excuses. Béa didn't even try to persuade me to stay, so flagrant and understandable must have been my reason for wanting to go. Nor, though, as yet, did she feel any need to beg indulgence for Sacha's conduct. She escorted me to the front door, leaving him sottishly slumped over the table. As we stood together on the threshold, and she held one slim arm high against the frame of the door, she asked where I was staying in Saint-Malo. I told her, and she replied that her husband would get in touch with me as soon as he returned from England.

'*Was* that Jean-Marc, by the way?' I asked.

She looked at me uncomprehendingly.

'Jean-Marc?'

'On the telephone?'

'Oh. Yes, it was. I'm sorry, I should have said, shouldn't I?

Yes, he was ringing to advise me to expect you in a couple of days. I told him you were already here.'

Then, after a pause: 'What can I say, Guy?'

'Say nothing. You weren't to blame.'

'Sacha isn't generally like that, you know. But he is what you English call accident-prone – except in his case the accidents always seem to happen to somebody else. And, as you probably guessed, he's just a little bit in . . .' She chose not to go on, so I never did find out whether what she intended to say was 'a little bit insane' or 'a little bit in love with me'.

She closed the door behind her. I searched for the keys to the Rolls. As I turned on the ignition, I heard a row exploding inside the villa, the kind of row that traditionally follows the leave-taking of an untimely guest, only very much louder and more vicious. At the same time, I was plagued by something else I had heard, but earlier, something that had been said in the dining room, something that had impressed me as not quite – how shall I put it? – not quite orthodox, and that I'd been in a position to put right – oh, but what had it been? And by whom had it been said? For a good long while, as I drove the Rolls through the streets of Saint-Malo, I worried at the thing. But it wasn't on the tip of my tongue or even close to settling upon it.

The remainder of the day was agony. I continued to feel like the odd man out at a dinner party. Everyone except me was having a good time, or seemed to be having a good time, or at the very least was pretending to have a good time. Everyone except me was passionately interested, or seemed to be passionately interested, or pretended to be passionately interested, in the *chemin de ronde* and the cathedral and the cute souvenir shops which I found myself fruitlessly circling again and again, to less and less purpose.

Even if I delayed for as long as I humanly could the hour of the evening meal, that regular-as-clockwork moment of truth for the solitary traveller, it was still only six o'clock when I dined in a cheap pizzeria, the self-styled Drug's Pizza. Afterwards I strolled down towards the beach. The heavens were on fire. A scalloped crest of cliffs extended southward along the Breton coast until it all but coalesced with the horizon. In the early evening light its serration looked both raw and spruce, like a row of thick-nibbed, freshly sharpened pencils in a pencil box. Two rowing boats had been tethered to a decrepit wooden jetty. Their twitchily unquiet moaning, as they tossed and turned in their sleep, was softer than silence itself.

There was no one at all on the beach at that hour, although the day's busy, feckless footprints still criss-crossed each other in a spectral pattering and patterning. Far above me gulls dipped and swooped, hugging the planet's airy shore. Feeling dreadfully pale, obtrusively British, I stepped on to the muddy sands and slowly walked my memories along them the way I might have walked a dog.

Later, in my room at the Apothéose, I lay flat out on the bed and lit a cigarette. A wisp of smoke, lazily twirling in on itself, spiralled upward as if I were projecting a film on the ceiling. I had left the window open and the street lighting had spun an intricate cobweb of shadows across the wall at my back. On a little table at my bedside sat my leather-encased travelling clock: it wasn't yet ten o'clock. Not ten o'clock — and here I was, back in my room, with only an Anthony Burgess novel for company. Under my window, four Italians, two married couples it sounded like, were volubly debating what to eat, and where. I stuffed a couple of *boules Quiès* in my ears.

Suddenly the telephone rang. It was the night receptionist. There was a lady asking for me in the foyer, a lady by the name of . . . (the night receptionist paused to learn the name I already knew it had to be) . . . Béatrice Cheret. She was eager to speak to me.

I slipped on my jacket, remembering only at the last minute to remove the *boules* from my ears, and ran downstairs. The object of the night receptionist's unembarrassed gaze, Béa was wearing a beltless and buttonless raincoat so long it nearly brushed the floor. She was leaning against a *faux-marbre* pillar, and it struck me that every time I'd seen her she'd been leaning against something or other. She had the instinct of a cat for squeezing up on the edge of things. A cat is never more content than when tucked into the little interstice of empty space that divides two cushions on a settee or stretched out along the slender gap that runs around the walls of a room between the carpet and the floor. And a cat was what Béa was like. I imagined her, in a one-piece bathing costume, basking on a southern shoreline, half of her body on the beach, half in the sea, a wave pouring in across the sand and gradually shading in the isosceles triangle of her tanned open legs. In some previous existence, I said to myself, and this was a woman who had had several previous existences, she had positively been a cat.

We demurely shook hands.

'I took a chance,' she said, raking her hair with her hand. 'I was sure you'd be out, but this was the only address I had for you.'

I was ashamed to be caught indoors so early in the evening.

'It's been a long day.'

'Are you exhausted?'

Thankful for small mercies, I took the bait.

'I'm all in.'

'I see.' She paused. 'Too all in to have a drink with me?'

'You mean now?'

'Why not?'

'Yes, why not,' I answered after a moment. 'Actually,' I said, 'actually I'd like that very much.'

'Shall we take the Rolls? I saw it parked outside. And I know a place where we can be alone.'

We drove westward out of Saint-Malo along a moonlit coastal road. It was flanked on one side by hills and forests and, on still higher hills, by venerable stone-walled farms, of which no more than the rooftops were visible; on the other side by the ocean, glassily calm save for some routine foamy turmoil around a miniature archipelago of bouldery islets and promontories that rose out of it like so many black icebergs. Béa, beside me, said scarcely a word as I drove, speaking at first only to give me directions and eventually saying nothing at all since there was only the coastal road ahead of me and hence nowhere else I could go. She sat as far away from me as she could, not, as I told myself, for any reason that ought to have concerned me but because the cushiony corner of the Rolls offered her body the sensual contact of two surfaces, the seat cover and the window, instead of just one. And she smoked. That was something else, I recalled, that I had almost always seen her doing – smoking.

She finally told me to stop, and I turned into the drive, already choked with parked cars, of a brightly neon-lit hotel.

This hotel had a bar, the Monna Vanna, dark and cool, the sole access to which was down a claustrophobic spiral staircase. Small, tubular, low-legged tables lined all four walls. Each of these tables was lit by a narcissistically elongated lamp, gangrenous and fey, freakish of form and acidic of colour, as if parodying a style that had never existed, an *art déco* that had evolved in the twenties and thirties of a universe whose civilisation was a warped parallel of our own. The seats were pouffes – oxblood red, *crème de cacao*, that sort of thing. There was just one other couple in the room, and, when I eventually succeeded in identifying it, I realised that the taped mood music was Poulenc's *Les Biches*, of all unlikely Muzak.

Our order was taken by the barman, a lisping young hunk

who greeted Béa by her given name. For twenty minutes or so thereafter she and I talked about nothing in particular, pleasantly, unmemorably, sipping our drinks. I ordered another two whiskies. This time the barman leaned right over the table in front of me to whisper sibilant nothings in Béa's ear. Playfully pushing him away, she lit yet another cigarette.

Exasperated by the barman's easy familiarity, emboldened by the whisky I wasn't supposed to drink, I watched her suck in a lungful of smoke.

'Don't you think you smoke too many cigarettes?' I said.

Béa stared at me for a few seconds.

'Why,' she finally said, all mock-innocence, 'I only smoke one at a time.' She flashed her eyes at me. 'But, you know, Guy,' she went on, 'you really are something of a – I don't know if you have a word for it in English – a *gaffeur*?'

'A *gaffeur*?'

'Well, think of it. First you accuse Sacha of being practically a criminal. Then you tell me – me, whom you met only this afternoon – that I smoke too much. So blunt, Guy, so to the point! Perhaps after all you aren't the classic stolid Englishman you appear to be.'

'I sincerely hope I'm not,' I replied, not quite bringing off the raffish tone I'd been aiming for, and I added that it hadn't been my intention to be rude. Obviously, it was none of my business how many cigarettes she smoked. As for the remark I'd made to Sacha at lunch, I had merely been trying to keep the conversation going.

'He doesn't make it easy,' I said.

'I know. That's why I came to see you at the hotel. I wanted to apologise for what happened today, really apologise. In a way I couldn't do in his presence. Besides, I'm like a doctor, I prefer to see my people one at a time.'

(My people?)

'I told you before, there's nothing to apologise for. But tell me,' I continued, 'who is he?'

'Who is who?'

'This Sacha. Who is he exactly?'

'He's Jean-Marc's partner. I thought you knew that.'

'I do. But that can't be all there is to him.'

'No?'

'Well, today, for example. Why did he get into the Rolls and drive it away instead of trying to find out what it was doing back in Saint-Malo? What kind of partner is that? There could have been a perfectly logical explanation. There *was* an explanation, even though it wasn't what you'd call perfectly logical. All he had to do was wait and ask.'

'I know.'

'And why does he behave the way he does? What did that look mean that he kept giving you at table?'

Béa smiled.

'What are you hinting at, Guy? That Sacha has some kind of malevolent hold over me?'

'No . . . But if it weren't such a laughable idea, I'd say he was jealous of me.'

'He is. He's jealous of everybody. It's his nature.'

There was something else I wanted to know.

'Does he live at the villa?'

Béa held her half-empty whisky glass up in front of her eyes – her eyes which, as I looked into that glass from my own half of the table, seemed to be swimming around inside it like two exotic little bluefins. She swallowed the whisky that was left and, rattling the ice like dice, waved the glass at the lisping barman as a signal for him to bring us the same again. Then she said, apropos of nothing, 'Do you know what's wrong with human relationships, Guy?'

'No, what?'

'It's that we marry our lovers when we should marry our friends. It's that basic. A love affair is a spasm. It's like a sneeze. You can't legalise a sneeze.'

I took what I thought was a cue.

'Why *did* you marry Jean-Marc?'

This time, though, I could see I'd caught her off guard.

'You know, Guy,' she eventually said, 'you're a little bit out of your depth here. You enter somebody's life, a life that was being lived a long, long time before you arrived on the scene, and after – what? – after two hours you think you've got the whole picture. Well, but you haven't, you see.'

I started to say something, but she interrupted me.

'You want to know about Jean-Marc and me? All right, I'll tell you. I really can't imagine why I should, but I will.'

What I was then to discover was that, save in name, Béa had long since ceased to be Jean-Marc's wife. They had married when she had been in her late teens. Jean-Marc had been a brilliant teacher at the Ecole des Beaux-Arts in Paris, by which she, of modest – indeed, if I could put faith in the picture she painted of them, peasant – Breton origins, had been employed as a part-time model.

'It's a cliché, I'm afraid, like something in Puccini, but these things do happen and it's no use turning up your nose. Naturally, I was grateful to Jean-Marc, but I did love him too. I was even in love with him. For a while . . . I think . . .' She made a charming moue. 'It's so hard to know now. All that was twelve years ago. For twelve years he's been grooming me – that's the word he likes to use for it. Grooming. And it's certainly been a success. When I look in the mirror, Guy, I'm two people, the person Jean-Marc thinks I am and somewhere, somewhere even now, all these years later, the person I myself know I am.'

'Just about everybody feels like that, you know. We're children dressed up in grown-ups' clothing.'

'Let's just say I couldn't go on being grateful all my life. There's a limit to the number of times you can say thank you to the same human being and still mean it.'

'And Sacha?'

'Sacha was there. That was Sacha's virtue. It was a question of timing. If there had been somebody else . . .' She didn't finish that sentence either but added, 'And that's all over, too, in case you were about to ask me.'

Am I, I couldn't resist putting to myself, am I going to fall in love with her? What a fantasy! It was absurd and it was puerile and yet . . . and yet, apart from the unique set of

circumstances of our meeting, the romantically corny lightning flash (fate's patented trademark, its tired old logo) and
the swapping of cars, my excuse, my sole excuse, for
thinking such a thought was the fact, the indisputable fact,
that we all of us lead a double life. No one can monitor our
loves and lusts. No one can set police dogs sniffing around
the insides of our brains. Sexual attraction is what cosmolo-
gists term a singularity. It's the black hole of the psyche,
where neither the priorities nor the proprieties of the realist
imperative any longer apply. In my head, at least, I could do
as I pleased.

We were on our third drinks. The lisping barman had
gone, and we were the only customers left in the bar. From
out of my reverie I heard Béa ask me if I was married.

Was I married? The whisky had made me brazen and
reckless. I so wanted to talk, to let myself go.

I paused, then:

'I was married,' I replied. 'But I killed my wife.'

'You killed your wife?' said Béa calmly, as if imitating my
own feigned dispassion.

It was the first time I had ever spoken about Ursula's death to
anyone outside the clinic's walls. My friends, of course,
didn't have to be told by me, and those who had visited me
in hospital never once raised the subject. I caught them
sometimes coming close, extremely close, but they would
always at the last shy off.

It had been an accident, a statistic, a banal New Year's Day statistic. The only part of it not banal was that I hadn't been drinking. Not a single glass of champagne, not a lager, nothing but the Perrier I had been nursing all through lunch. Ursula had actually complained that I was overdoing things and, on the drive home, her head reposing on my shoulder, she was half-tipsily making the point again when it happened. It was on the border between Sussex and Hampshire, near a layby, at about four o'clock in the afternoon – I had just pointed out to her the layby's cracked wooden signpost, snow-topped, as I remarked, like a drop-cap *T* in one of Dickens's Christmas stories. It was there and then that I'd first had the dream that wasn't a dream, that I'd first heard the vulpine howl of skidding tyres and seen the arch of trees above us, seen the snowman in the field, fainting in the sun like a guardsman on parade, seen Ursula's face at the point of impact, Ursula's face on which I had turned to gaze, helplessly, as it started to fissure into an unendurable network of crazy-paving cracks.

'When was this?'

'When?' I had to think. 'Fourteen months ago.'

Fourteen months. I had spent the last fourteen months in what used to be called – in a euphemism which has now utterly forfeited the tenderising faculty it could once lay claim to – an institution. Fourteen months ago I had voluntarily committed myself. I had agreed to sign an allegedly optional admission form, although that was something I didn't at first want to do and had to be coaxed into.

'It's just a piece of paper,' the clinic's director had said – clinically, the word has to be – as he held out his Biro.

So is a death sentence, I remember thinking.

But I was wrong. The clinic was a splendid place, located on the Sussex Downs and surrounded by National Trust land – dense forestry mostly, although the only trees in the clinic's own gardens were palms as impeccable as aigrettes. Its windows were heavily lidded by turquoise blinds, like those of a Manhattan town house, and looked out over an eight-acre estate in which none of the inmates save myself ever seemed to care to walk. It had a cricket pitch, a billiard room and a staff of nurses in whom the relief and gladness of having landed on their feet in private practice were almost tangible. They never left me to myself, these nurses, parading through my room every other minute of the day, taking my blood pressure, samples of my urine, dropping everything they were doing if I so much as cleared my throat, even accompanying me, hand in hand, stark naked as I was, into my *en suite* bathroom and helping me up three little steps into the tub itself.

A psychotherapist, a Dr Loder, had been assigned to me. He was a small man, always nattily turned out, usually in a cashmere cardigan and a hairy, thickly knotted woollen tie, unlike most of the hospital's staff, who tended to settle for a kind of easygoing, simpatico slovenliness.

To begin with, he did all the talking. He would blithely ramble on about anything which popped into his head. I remember monologues on Marvell's poetry, on George du

Maurier's novels, on fly-fishing expeditions to wild Highland streams, on the very few London hotels that could still rustle up a goodly high tea (his turn of phrase) and on God knows what else. I remember, too, that of all the staff he alone apparently was permitted to keep a pet on the premises, a fox terrier, a pup, male, with an adolescently floppy tread and a quartet of downy white paws which gave it a droll preppy appearance and made me think of some lanky, loose-limbed Ivy League athlete in white ankle socks. Its name was Mao, a wistful sop, I imagine, to a decade in which Loder's younger self had aspired to change the world, and I would frequently run into both of them, out for a jolly constitutional (another Loderism) in the clinic's grounds.

For much of my stay, my sedated brain had no real notion of what Loder was talking about and I'd go to bed as bewildered by the state of my mind as when I'd wakened the same morning. Yet, perhaps for just that reason, his ram-shackle regime actually started to work. Perhaps I started to 'respond' (as my report card, which I sneaked an unauthor-ised look at, had it) because in my addled condition I found it hard to deliver myself of the belief that Loder wasn't a doctor at all but some genial old cove in whose company I'd chanced to find myself – in a pub, perhaps, or in the litter-strewn waiting room of a railway station – and whose purpose in ranging over such sundry subjects of conversation was less to 'cure' me of anything than simply, faced with my sulky autism, to fill in my antisocial silences. If in the end I did 'open up', as Loder himself was fond, too fond, of describing my response to his treatment (which is probably why I now handle the formulation, which expresses nothing of what I was really going through, with the protective oven gloves of quotation marks), it was for no other reason than that I couldn't any longer tolerate having him carry the entire weight of our chats by himself. Session by session, I got back into the habit of talking — and talking, at last, about Ursula's death.

Thomas Mann writes somewhere of 'getting used to not getting used to' things. Well, when I left that clinic, only days before setting out for Brittany, I most certainly didn't feel 'cured' of anything, but perhaps I was beginning to get used to not getting used to my breakdown — to my insomnia, my dreams, my dizzy spells, my debilitating apathy. Perhaps I was beginning to feel cured of not feeling cured.

'Or doesn't that mean anything?'

I turned to Béa, who had been listening to me without saying anything, without even lighting a cigarette, than which I could have asked for no more convincing evidence of her absorption in the tale I'd had to tell her.

'It means it was an accident — and you needed fourteen months to understand that it was an accident.'

'An accident? What has that got to do with whether I feel guilty or not?'

'Do you feel guilty? You didn't murder her, after all.'

I looked up from my empty glass.

'How do you know?'

A pause.

'Well, did you?'

Another pause.

'Yes,' I said thoughtfully. 'Yes, I do feel as if I murdered her.'

She took my hand. Without saying a word, my fingertips tingling with electricity at contact with her palm, I let myself be led back up the spiral staircase with the obedient docility of a child, through the deserted hotel lobby and out into the car park.

Silently, from either side, we got in the Rolls. Installing myself in the driver's seat, I watched her slide nimbly in – and went on, for longer than I meant to, watching her. She returned my gaze with her own.

'A penny for your thoughts, Guy. No, forget it . . .' she immediately added – and, with her two hands, she coquettishly felt her breasts, her stomach, her hips, making believe she was searching for a coin – '. . . I don't have a penny on me.'

I stopped the engine which I had already started. Béa curled up at my side, cupping her uplifted knees with her arms, the tips of her elegantly shod toes apoise on the edge of the seat. We embraced with such violence I had the sense that ghostly negative imprints of her heart, her throat, her entrails, would forever after be stamped on mine and mine on hers. We riddled each other's faces, our lips, our brows, our cheeks, our necks, with kisses. Deafened by the ecstatic hum of my own passion, I heard nothing, only saw Béa mouthing 'More! More!' whenever, surfacing for air, I fleetingly let her lips be. It felt as if we were skiing on velvet, skiing on runny milk chocolate.

Then, as abruptly as it had begun, it was over. The silence was rent by a scream.

Béa was looking not at me but beyond me. I turned my head in line with hers, and what I saw through the car window, as if on an X-ray plate, was the skeleton of a face, its eyes two depthless shadows marooned in a sickly sea of pallor. There was a nose, too, plastered flat against the window pane.

I pulled myself away from Béa and opened the door. Shrinking back in fright, the face disappeared as swiftly as, so long ago, the blip of the Rolls had disappeared from my Mini's windscreen, but the two eyes continued to burn into mine. They belonged to Sacha. His features were ashen, monochromatic, as haunted as those of some pre-war film idol's. I reached out towards him, whether to repel or console the man I cannot now say. For, just as I made my move, we both heard Béa's voice from inside the Rolls.

'*Sacha!* Oh mon Dieu, mais qu'est-ce que tu es en train de faire? Tu m'espionnes maintenant?'

That voice, so altogether devoid of warmth, of affection, of even the normal human compassion that might just have done the trick, compassion that I myself momentarily felt for him, had a truly frightful effect on Sacha. He turned upon me a countenance that I hadn't expected, one not of loathing but of the most total helplessness and despair, and produced a bizarre, biscuity noise between his lips: he was grinding his teeth. We remained facing one another for a few seconds. Then he took flight. Before I could nab him – if that's what I had in mind when I stretched out my arm – his strange skinny silhouette, cloaked in an outsized black suit that was darker somehow than the pitch darkness by which it was cloaked in its turn, could be seen flapping against the sky like that of a scarecrow in mourning. (It came back to me that I'd already wondered, at the Villa Lazarus, whether he might be afflicted with some rare disorder of motoric articulation or coordination.)

I started to go after him until, from inside the Rolls, I heard Béa cry out impatiently, 'Guy! Guy, get back in the car, please. We have to catch up with him. You don't realise what he's capable of.'

I hurriedly slipped into the Rolls.

'Start the car, quick. And, Guy,' she said, pressing my steering-wheel hand, 'unless you never want to see me again – *ever* – you must back me up in everything I say and do. You understand? No matter how it pains you.'

I nodded.

'Yes, I understand. But –'

'Just start the car.'

We drove off in absurd pursuit – absurd, because it took us all of thirty seconds to overtake the poor man, whose hiccoughing progress, this way and that, caused him hardly to stray from the spot where the Rolls had been parked. And when we drew up alongside him, near an unkept, unkempt grass verge, he seemed meanwhile to have been both amplified and reduced to more human proportions – he was a man, like any other. On sight of him, on sight of his all too evident distress, I once more felt a perverse surge of sympathy.

Sacha refused at first to get into the car, even when Béa coolly pointed out that he couldn't possibly return home on foot. She wheedled and pleaded with him and told him not to be so temperamental: we'd all sit down and talk about it together like the civilised grown-ups that we were. She dropped enigmatic allusions to a shared past from which I was barred – some of which were tender, others, to my ears, less so – and I could see him start to weaken, even though he continued to glare at me with the venom I remembered from our very first meeting. Finally, when speech had done all it could, Béa leaned past my shoulders and opened one of the Rolls's rear doors. Although still shaking with rage, Sacha got in and we returned to Saint-Malo.

Inside the blue-and-coral salon Béa lit a new cigarette, drawing its smoke deep down into her throat. I sat stiffly in an armchair. Sacha – who wouldn't take a seat, who wouldn't be served a drink – stood in front of us both, obscuring the Balthus above the mantelpiece.

'Listen, Sacha,' said Béa, stubbing her no more than half-smoked Dunhill into a chunky, blurry-greeny-bluey glass ashtray that resembled a miniature Bel-Air swimming pool, 'I drove to Guy's hotel for one reason, and one reason only –

to offer him my excuses for the disgraceful scene at lunch. That's all we talked about. I felt I owed him an apology.'

I picked up two lies there. Sacha, though, leapt only on the first of them.

'So,' he said, looking at Béa, then at me, then at Béa again. 'You drove to his hotel, did you? In what? In the Rolls?'

'No, of course not,' she answered without missing a beat. 'How could I? Guy has had the car all day, as you know. I rang for a taxi.'

'I see,' said Sacha. 'I see. You got a taxi to take you twenty kilometres out of town on the chance that he' – pointing at me – 'might be in his room?'

'No,' said Béa in a heroically patient voice. 'I called Guy to apologise and he invited me to come out and have a drink with him. I accepted. Why – shouldn't I have?'

I racked my brain to recall the name of the hotel to which Béa had directed me in the Rolls and of which, I now learned, I was supposed to be a resident, but for the life of me I couldn't.

'And inside the car?' asked Sacha with a sneer. 'Is that what you call offering your excuses?'

'That', said Béa, 'was just one of those things that happen. Guy knows he means nothing to me.'

Listening to her, I told myself that Béa had to say what she did, that she had given me advance warning of her strategy. Still . . .

Sacha now turned in my direction.

'Et la clé,' he said, spraying me with French monosyllables, 'ça vous dit quelque chose?'

It was the third time that day I'd heard them refer to some 'key'.

'La clé? Quelle clé? De quoi vous parlez tous les deux?'

'La clé de la tour.'

I looked at both of them in turn, suddenly aware that I was alone of the three of us in not knowing what Sacha was talking about. In this matter at least Béa was on *his* side.

'What's this all about? I've no knowledge of any key. Or any tower. Will one of you please explain?'

There was a pause; but, instead of answering me, Béa asked Sacha whether he was now prepared to accept that his suspicions had been unfounded.

He stared at her for an eternity. Then, almost with regret, he shook his head.

'Trop tard, Béa, trop tard. Même si je m'efforçais de te croire, même si tu ne lui as rien dit – après cette petite scène révoltante je ne pourrais plus te faire confiance. Plus jamais.' At which point he reverted to English, as if to be sure that I would understand him. 'But you'll see, you'll both see. I've taken precautions.'

Flushing, Béa instinctively let her eyes dart around the salon.

'What have you done now?'

Sacha said nothing.

'God, what an idiot you can be! No, I was the idiot. I was

the idiot to have believed I could count on you. It's finished, you realise that − it's all over. Everything.'

Sacha turned white − there was that hangdog expression once more, that expression of inconsolable misery, his lower lip wobbling like a scolded child's. Then, a moment later, with his customary jerky, puppety gait, he stalked out of the room.

Not more than a couple of minutes after that, we heard the noise of a car rumbling down the villa's driveway and out into the street. Béa walked to the window and drew a curtain aside. I looked at her questioningly.

'It's nothing. I know him. He'll be back tomorrow.'

Following Sacha's departure there was a curious hush in the room, a calm-after-rather-than-before-the-storm sort of hush, and for a while we exchanged not a word. Neither Béa nor I knew what, if anything at all, we had to say to each other. I inferred from her silence that she was still thinking through what had just happened, so I didn't trouble her with the several questions that were troubling me. But when at last she did speak, it was merely to propose that we have a drink. I asked her once more, Sacha having gone and things calmed down, what it was all about, this talk of keys and towers. With a tomboyish pout, she replied that it was nothing, nothing at least she could talk about.

I said that I would have a whisky − and I added that I hoped she knew she could depend upon me if she should happen to be in any real trouble. But she may not have taken those last words in, for she had already left for the kitchen, from inside which I heard the sound of a refrigerator door opening and, a moment later, ice cubes being cracked out of their rubber hive, one of them skittering across the kitchen table and plopping on to the floor. Then there was silence.

After a few minutes of waiting for her, I got up and walked along the hallway into the kitchen. On a table that jutted out from one of its walls and sliced the spotless space in even halves, sat an enamel tray and a pair of crystal tumblers filled with ice cubes, but no whisky bottle. My guess was that Béa had gone elsewhere in the villa to find one.

I made my way back into the salon and sat down on a sofa in front of a glass coffee table that was nearly coterminous with it, the sofa itself being as long as a Hawaiian bar. I sat there, smoking, thinking, thinking and smoking – exhaling the smoke from one nostril and my thoughts, as it were, from the other. Perplexed as I already was by the sequence of events of the preceding twenty-four hours, I had no idea at all what was going to happen next and my temples were beginning to throb uncontrollably. I contemplated in turn, without thinking too much about what I was doing, the chic colour-coding of the salon's fittings; the Balthus over the mantelpiece (a real beauty); the clutter of eighteenth-century conversation pieces all hung up together at the fireside as if they ought to have been part of some larger painting with a museum setting, perhaps; and then, at last, the glass tabletop directly in front of me. On this table sat a cumbrous silver cigarette lighter in the shape of Aladdin's lamp. A vase of elegantly scrawny catkins, probably artificial. A pile of four album-sized books, whose spines had been aligned to run exactly parallel to one another (although the titles on those spines were displayed upside down, I found them easy enough to decode: *Robert Mapplethorpe*, *Christian Bérard*, *Hans Bellmer* and, the trickiest, *L'Histoire de la Peinture en Trompe l'Oeil*). And then I noticed, as far on the left of the table as they were on the right, another beautiful albumy book, open at a monochrome illustration half-covered by a folded-up copy of *Le Figaro* and a gold-leaf fountain pen lying neatly aslant it.

Why, I could not have said, but it was on that particular configuration of objects that my eyes definitively came to rest. It was on them too — and, again, who knows why? — that I suddenly decided to perform a bit of fancy focus-pulling, causing most of the room to become a blur and only the book, the pen and the *Figaro* to stand out from the now out-of-focus background. But that still wasn't sufficiently close for me. Something compelled me to sit up properly — by this time I was lounging on the sofa — and draw even nearer.

The middle half of the illustration, I repeat, was covered by the newspaper and the fountain pen and I could now see that, running parallel underneath it, there was a similarly obscured caption, only the first and last words of which were legible. I read them. To the left of the *Figaro* there were two: 'La' and 'Clé', and to the right there were three: 'de La Tour'.

La Clé de La Tour. The Key of the Tower.

With a quiver of apprehension, I repeated the five words inwardly, in both English and French. Then I sat bolt upright and, sweeping the pen to one side with a careless wingstroke, slowly lifted the copy of *Le Figaro*. The illustration that it had been covering, and that took up a full double-page spread of the book, was of a glossy black-and-white reproduction of a painting. And now that the *Figaro* and the fountain pen had been withdrawn, its caption could be read *in toto*. It was: '*La Clé de Vair*' by *Georges de La Tour*.

The painting depicted two figures, both of them cropped at the midriff. The figure on the left, from the viewer's perspective, was a beardless young man, ringleted, snub-nosed and pasty-complexioned, with a hint of eunuchoid corpulence about his half-seen body and a pronounced air of having been drawn from stock – he was not, in short, all that credible a human being, given the painter's fame, and much less skilfully rendered in facial features than in dress. He wore a pleated beret topped by an ostrich plume as homely and ethereal as a puff of pipe smoke, a dark velvet tunic with fiendishly complex, painstakingly painted shoulder knots, and a waistcoat picked out in a colourful royal-hunt motif, all gorgeously accoutred courtiers on horseback and greyhounds coiled like bedsprings. On his left – which is to say, on my right – was a woman. Her features, however, it was more difficult to distinguish, as, in her left hand, she held a candle which, casting a glow from beneath over the lower half of her perfectly oval face, had the effect of neutralising the modelling that would otherwise have articulated it. Her hair, ash-blonde, was held fast inside a chignon from which the odd strand and kiss-curl obtruded on to her deathly white forehead; her long-lashed eyes were in profile, in a manner of speaking, slanting sideways towards her male companion; and her mouth was ever so slightly ajar, as if she had just said something of import to him. She was the more starkly dressed of the two, wearing a plain robe with a maidenly semi-circular neckline, its sole adornment a sash bedecked with jade and pearls, a sash which dazzled less than it might have done because of the shadows hovering like moths about the candle's eerie underglow. These human figures apart, there were, in the exiguous space, not much roomier than that of a monk's cell, in which La Tour had portrayed them, and which was illuminated only by the woman's candle, just two further compositional elements of note: a door, whose gnarled wooden knob was perceptible behind the figure of the young man; and what was either a window or else a miniaturised landscape – painted in a discordantly morbid and overwrought style reminiscent of El Greco – of an island surfacing from a curdling ocean and tapering onward and upward to form a rocky black conelet. On the uppermost point of that rock, planted there like a mountaineer's flag, was a stone tower of elementary design and absolutely no pragmatic utility, being both doorless and windowless.

Actually, there was one other detail, and the most significant of all; so subtly done was it, however, it took me several seconds of careful perusal before I managed to spot it.

With her right hand the woman was surreptitiously passing to her companion (although why surreptitiously? for, not counting the painter himself, there was no one else present in the room to apprehend them *in flagrante* whatever it was the two of them were up to) a small pouch or purse in miniver fur whose open ends were drawn together by a finicky tasselled bowstring. From its shape and its size and the asymmetric indentations on its surface, it was obvious that this pouch or purse contained a key.

Underneath the caption there was a boxed-in chronicle of the painting's somewhat *mouvementé* past. Fascinated, I read:

La Tour's 'La Clé de Vair' was almost certainly painted in the early 1640s, as is clear from two details of internal evidence. In the first place, it is signed by the artist (in Latin) in the left-hand margin, whereas, as we have already seen, no signatures figured on any of La Tour's earliest paintings. In the second place, and even if less assured an example than he would later achieve in the same genre, it indubitably belongs among the mysterious series of 'night pictures' initiated, as is generally accepted, by 'The Payment of Dues', now in the Lvov Museum. It is true, to be sure, that the date of the latter painting has always been a vexed question, since, although the painted record of a year is visible alongside the signature, only its first two numbers, unmistakably '16', are decipherable; and the attribution – by the Soviet art historian, and dedicated admirer of La Tour, Yuri Zolotov – of 16(41) or 16(42) continues to remain an open question. Nevertheless, it being so observably redolent of 'The Payment of

Dues' in style, technique and composition, it seems unquestionable that 'La Clé de Vair' either immediately predated it in the canon or, as is likelier, followed it by no more than a year or two.

Nothing is known of the canvas's original provenance – notably, who commissioned it and, given its ambiguous iconography, why – and the first trace of its existence surfaced in the early nineteenth century when it was recorded, in the state archives, as an item in the collection of Ivan Domsky (1761–1829), a Muscovite nobleman, who is known to have subsequently donated it to the Lyubomirsky Museum in St Petersburg in 1824 (which once also housed 'The Payment of Dues'). Although he was indifferent to the artist's name – he nowhere cites it – Turgenev made references (only passing ones, unfortunately) to the picture in two of the essays in art criticism which he wrote in the 1880s: thus we may assume that it probably remained in the museum's collection until the Revolution of 1917. From then on, however, there is no further public record of 'La Clé de Vair' in Russia – or, as of course it was henceforth to be known, the Soviet Union – and, indeed, no further corroboration of the painting's very existence until 1937, the year in which the above photograph was taken.

It was established, virtually simultaneously, by Zolotov and the distinguished Parisian dealer Pierre Rosenberg that the photographer in question was one Mikaël Duphin of Caen, now deceased. Duphin, alas, kept very few records of work commissioned and carried out; his studio, situated in the Rue Lorraine in Caen, has long since been razed; and his sole surviving descendant, a daughter now resident in Geneva, has no recall of *the circumstances in which the painting might have been photographed.*

Thus, ignoring the not necessarily trustworthy catalogue of the Lyubomirsky Museum (which, in accordance with an unofficial or semi-official practice adopted by several Russian museums, may well have gone on listing it as an acquisition after it had in fact disappeared from the permanent collection), it can be stated with assurance only that the last recorded sighting of 'La Clé de Vair', a work representative of a crucial stage in La Tour's development, was in 1885, with the newspaper publication of Turgenev's essays. Regretfully, it has to be assumed that it is now forever lost to us.

Guarding the place with my thumb, I shut the volume and studied, first, the spine – the publisher, I remarked, was the Porlock Press in Cambridge (Cambridge, England, not Cambridge, Massachusetts) – and then the cover. The title was *The Pictorial Art of the Seventeenth Century* and the author one Alexandre Liebermann. There was no snapshot or potted biography of this author among the book's endpapers, so I flipped it back open and peered again at the reproduction.

As my eyes roamed over it, I felt the veins in my temples pulsate. There was something about this painting that disturbed me – something about it – something I couldn't entirely –

'Eh bien. You have found the key.'

I started. Béa was standing in front of me, bearing on a bamboo tray the pair of iced tumblers I had seen on the kitchen table – chaperoned, now, by a half-full bottle of Johnnie Walker. (And, I might add in parenthesis, it occurred to me that it had taken her an unaccountably long time to find and fetch that bottle. Had she, I wondered, had she been *willing* me to chance upon this book – lying as it was, exposed, so obligingly exposed, at the relevant page? Close brackets, I said to myself, but keep an open mind.)

She set the tray down on the coffee table, making what space she could for it amid the flotilla of objects – books, cigarette lighter, vase of catkins – already at anchor on its surface. I watched her attentively, dumbly, waiting to bring her face to face with the evidence. There is a moment when one's about to sink into a deckchair and one can physically lower oneself no further and one has to *let go*, one has to entrust oneself to the air and the chair and the principle that when one has traversed the former the latter will still be loyally there to catch one. In my dealings with Béa, that moment had come.

Jabbing a finger at the reproduction, I said, 'That's *la clé de la tour*, isn't it?'

Béa nodded – and, again, I had the feeling that she was willing me on, wanting me to know that I was getting warm, nodding not only in acknowledgment of what I had already found out but as if encouraging me on to ever further revelations, drawing each new fragment of truth out of me as, clue by clue, some general-knowledge staple – please sir, 1066 – may be drawn out of a schoolchild.

'Which means,' I continued, 'that it isn't lost, that it exists. Doesn't it?'

A pause.

'Doesn't it?'

Another silent nod from Béa.

'I heard you, in this room, this very morning, tell Sacha to go and look for the key – *va chercher la clé*, those were your exact words – which means that it, the key . . . no, I mean the painting, was somewhere inside the villa . . . No, I'm wrong again, because Sacha went *outside* to fetch it. That's it . . . that must be it! The canvas must have been somewhere inside the car, inside the Rolls.'

A nod.

'So the painting – which exists – was in the Rolls . . . Yet . . .' (red hot) '. . . it was at Jean-Marc's own suggestion that he and I exchange cars, which means that *he* didn't know. He couldn't have known that it was in the Rolls, or he'd never have made the swap. But you knew . . . you and Sacha, Sacha Liebermann, Alexandre Liebermann, you both knew the painting was there.' (A Georges de La Tour – I'd been tootling around Saint-Malo with a priceless Georges de La Tour in the back, or wherever it had been concealed, of my car.)

Béa poured us out a whisky apiece and forced mine into my hand.

'Chin-chin,' she said matter-of-factly, swallowing her own.

I sipped the whisky without enthusiasm and waited for her

to speak. And it was quite a story she told me. What I had to understand, she insisted, was the nature of her relationship with Jean-Marc. From comments of hers made back at the Monna Vanna I had extrapolated that, their physical desire for each other having ebbed into the relaxed mutual inappetence which is liable to overtake every long-term union sooner or later, theirs had become, in the most literal sense of the phrase, a marriage of convenience. In actual fact, as I would now discover to my surprise, Béa *loathed* Jean-Marc. For it appeared that he at least had never lost his appetite for her, and she had long since reached the point where she couldn't stomach his petting and pawing of her, his vetting of the company she kept, the clothes she wore, the very dreams she dreamed.

When I asked her, half-jokingly, if what she was claiming was that Jean-Marc had 'bought' her, she replied simply: 'Yes.' He had bought her just as he had bought his Rolls, and his paintings, and everything he had ever had in his life. And gradually she had begun to grope for an exit from Hell.

It was Sacha who showed her the way out, Sacha a.k.a. Alexandre Liebermann, a world-renowned expert on seventeenth-century French art and the author of the book that was still lying, between Béa and myself, on the coffee table. Sacha frequently had canvases brought to him by private individuals for evaluation. And one of these canvases, owned by a Normand couple in their sixties – he the quintessential French provincial *notaire*, she the shy type, visibly embarrassed at the notion of wasting so grand an expert's time, not to mention, and she duly didn't, their own good money, on what, she was persuaded, was a third-rate daub they had been using to conceal the door of a wall-safe in the *notaire*'s library – was 'La Clé de Vair'. After a few minutes of close study, Sacha realised that the canvas should have been in the safe, not guarding it. It was worth infinitely more than anything the *notaire* and his wife might have squirrelled away for their twilight years. Although he had never seen it in the flesh, he knew instantly what it was – why, he had actually cited it in his book. Over the centuries so many of La Tour's canvases had gone missing, presumed lost forever, but maybe just mislaid. This was by no means the only case of such a windfall.

The selfsame day, Sacha had frantically driven up the coast from his studio and related the whole story to Béa. And in that windfall she saw at once and at last an opportunity to crawl out from underneath the tombstone of her own life.

'I was at the end of my tether. I would have done anything. Don't judge me too harshly.'

'Béa, I don't intend to judge you at all.'

Now came the ticklish part. Béa confessed that it had been her idea to buy the painting at a knockdown price from its bemused and poorly primed owners – albeit not so knockdown as to arouse their suspicions. In fact, she and Sacha were prepared to pay thirty thousand francs for it, a handsome amount by most standards if far from a fair deal for an authentic Georges de La Tour. Monsieur and Madame Notaire didn't suspect a thing, were on the contrary gushingly appreciative and accepted without hesitation. Sacha's name and probity were after all unimpeachable, they had never read his book, they were in all likelihood not even aware of its existence, and his stated reason for acquiring the painting — as he described it to them, a goodish if scrappy copy of one of Caravaggio's French epigones — was his passion for every type and quality of the period's art.

'But why would Sacha risk his reputation on such a fraud?'

'He wouldn't at first,' replied Béa. 'I had to persuade him.'

'And how did you do that?'

Béa paused, then said, 'Well, what do you think? I went to bed with him.'

'I see.'

'Sacha was in love with me. He'd been in love with me since he started to work for Jean-Marc. I wasn't interested, but that didn't stop Jean-Marc from suspecting us two. I sometimes think he kept Sacha on not just because he was irreplaceable — he knows a hell of a lot more about painting than Jean-Marc has ever done — but also because he wanted to test us. As though, if he *were* to dismiss him, he'd never know whether we really were having an affair. The one way to trap us was to keep Sacha around, even if it meant that the chance of catching us at something would be all the greater. And sometimes, long before the La Tour, I'd actually been tempted to put Sacha out of his misery and go to bed with him — just to prove Jean-Marc right. There are two ways of acting on an unjustified reputation. You can either deny it — or you can justify it. Guy, I *had* denied it, I had denied it

time and time again, and that hadn't worked, so I was ready
to justify it when "La Clé de Vair" turned up. Which, I
suppose, settled it.'

'Of course it did.'

'You promised you wouldn't judge.'

'I won't, I won't. Go on.'

Well, now they had this masterwork by La Tour on their
hands and, for the next month or so, they weren't quite sure
what they ought to do about it. One thing they did know:
the painting could never be sold on the open market. Even if
the poor Notaires were incapable of recognising its true
value, it could not be subjected to the scrutiny of the art
world. If ever word of its survival got out, there would be
the most horrendous tug-of-war among the various interested and indignant parties: the Russian authorities (not to
mention their French counterparts); the Lyubomirsky
Museum; the descendants, should they chance to be intact
and extant, of Ivan Domsky; and, bringing up the rear but in
there nevertheless fighting their doomed corner, the two
Normand dodos who had been so enchanted with their
thirty thousand francs. The irony was that the problem,
already a treacherous one, had been compounded by Sacha
himself when he wrote about the painting in his book.

But there was to be a second and even nicer irony. It was
Jean-Marc who, quite unintentionally, provided the eventual
solution. One of his wealthiest clients was a Lebanese
industrialist who lived a plush reclusive life in a palatial
country mansion in the English Home Counties – in Kent,

Béa thought it was – a house dripping with the canvases of Old Masters and *petits-maîtres*. Born a billionaire, from a cosmopolitan fleet of oil tankers he had inherited from his father, he was, according to Jean-Marc, not exactly the black sheep but, if such a thing exists, the grey sheep of the family. Wishing for nothing else than to be left alone to gloat over his accumulation of goodies, he had, where the company that bore his name was involved, authority without power, his attendance at meetings required solely when there were papers to be signed. Again according to Jean-Marc, Nasr (the client's name) signed a lot of papers, occasionally in his (Jean-Marc's) presence. Some he read, some he didn't, but it didn't seem to make too much difference either way. These papers would be spirited from his desk, before the ink had dried on his signature, by a pair of goateed Arab operators in Armani suits who then melted out of his life, only to reappear a month later with an attaché case of fresh papers to sign. The periods between signing sessions Nasr would spend hanging and rehanging, like so many trophies, his Légers and Modiglianis, Corots and Renoirs. And such an obsession had his collection of artworks become, it was Béa's conviction that, like several other clients of Jean-Marc she could name, he would not be too scrupulous about the provenance and precise legal status of an original Georges de La Tour if there was a chance of getting his hands on it.

She was right. Sacha was quietly dispatched to sound Nasr out; and, just as she had foreseen, when the latter was shown a photograph of the painting, he immediately had to have it.

It all went amazingly well to plan. They were offered ten million pounds sterling for the original, one tenth of which was to be deposited in a numbered bank account in Zurich, the balance to be paid on delivery.

Delivery. Here, like many a tyro before them, they made the mistake of being a little too crafty for their own good. Although customs checks were still being upheld by the vigilant and mildly xenophobic British, they were a much more offhand affair than in the old, pre-European Union days. It would have been simpler, and it might have been wiser, for Sacha – since Béa herself couldn't make a move without Jean-Marc wanting to know where, why and for whom – to have flown into Heathrow and trotted through the usually unattended customs hall with the rolled-up cylinder of 'La Clé de Vair' under his arm. Yet the canvas was no miniature, nor was Sacha any stranger to paranoia; and it was he who, at last, came up with the notion of concealing it inside the Rolls, in a hollow compartment under the back seat, and having the Lebanese simply summon Jean-Marc to Kent for a conference. On his arrival, the canvas would be plucked out of the car behind his back, the conference would be agreeably lubricated but turn out, not for the first time, to be inconclusive – or else Nasr might ask Jean-Marc to purchase for him some minor, uncostly painting which had genuinely come on the market. It would all have gone off without a hitch had not a stray bolt of lightning struck a plane tree, stranding Guy and Jean-Marc on either side of it.

When Sacha saw the Rolls back in town, he naturally believed that their scheme had gone calamitously wrong – 'and,' sighed Béa, '– and you know the rest.'

'Then that was Jean-Marc you talked to on the phone at lunchtime?' I asked, forgetting that I'd already posed the same question earlier that afternoon.

'Why no, it wasn't,' said Béa, giving me a different answer this time. 'It was Nasr himself. He was ringing to inform me of the situation. I was afraid you would have guessed it couldn't be Jean-Marc, because I called him "vous", not "tu".'

'I had guessed,' I replied, 'except that I didn't know I had.' (So that was what had been nagging at me all day.)

I poured myself another drink. Béa stood over me, in front of the Balthus, studying the effect on me of what she had just said. Somewhere to the right of us, out of eyeshot, the silence was tempered by the growlingly loud tick-tock of a mantelpiece clock.

'You haven't forgotten what you said?'

'What I said?'

'That I could always depend upon you.'

' "If you're ever in any real trouble" is what I said.'

'But I am in trouble, don't you see. Nasr is suspicious. Frankly, I don't think he believed the business about the lightning.'

'I'm not surprised. Except that it's true, it *is* unbelievable.' Then I added, flatly, almost mechanically, certainly unconvincingly, 'Listen, Béa, the only course left to you and Sacha is to return the money you've already been paid. Believe me, there is no other solution.'

'You won't help me?'

'Help you? You realise what it is you're asking? That I be an accessory to a crime.'

Béa knelt on the rug before me and I felt her tanned hands trembling as they clasped mine.

'What can ten million pounds possibly mean to this Nasr creature? I've told you, he's a billionaire. Not a millionaire – a *billionaire*.' She shook her head. 'Anyway, it's too late to turn back. He won't allow us not to sell the painting to him, not now he's had a whiff of it. And even if he did, what are Sacha and I supposed to do with it then? Aren't you forgetting that a crime has already been committed – when we bought the painting for thirty thousand francs. We can't get out of that.'

'Yes you can. What Sacha has to do is admit that, when he examined the canvas, he realised too late that it was a genuine La Tour, and return it to the couple he bought it from.'

'Admit that he failed to identify a La Tour – Sacha Liebermann, the historian, the connoisseur! Who would believe that? His reputation would be in ruins. And when Jean-Marc found out, which he would, my life wouldn't be worth living.'

She knelt even nearer, violating my air space. Her eyes were now so close to mine, they felt closer to me than my own. It was as if her body had gained a whole new dimension to be explored; as if my own body, too, by a harmoniously timed effect of simultaneity, had gained a whole marvellous new set of sensory equipment with which to explore it. The next words she spoke brushed against – what am I saying, they all but kissed – my lips.

'Listen to me, Guy,' she whispered. 'This is my chance and it can be yours too. Your life can begin over again. Just think of it – ten million pounds. Everything you always wanted is now yours.' She repeated – but this time, as I darkly dared imagine, she wasn't repeating herself at all but making me a different kind of promise – 'Everything.'

'And you, Béa? What about you and Sacha?'

'That's over, I swear. It never was very much of anything, to be honest. But, whatever it was, it's over now.'

I looked into her upturned face. Then, taking advantage of the silence left suspended by her last words, I drew her down towards me on the divan, tenderly at first, then brutally, almost boorishly, yet all the while lavishing my hunger for her on her eyes, on her eyelashes, on those long, fine, countable lashes which I craved to caress one by one. And, slowly, but with surprising ease and unselfconsciousness, I resurrected the rusty, never-to-be-forgotten cadences of foreplay.

The night had spread two thick smears of butter over my closed eyelids. I burrowed as deep into my pillow as if it were a cloud, as if my head with its butter-coated eyelids might gloriously mine its way through to the pillow's reverse half, the half still nestled in darkness. I turned over on my other side. I must briefly have opened an eye in mid-pendulum, however, for I caught sight of a blue lampshade I didn't recall having seen before and, on the other side of the room, a framed landscape of a Venetian regatta, sequinned with highlights, a photo or possibly a Canaletto, my vision was still too fuzzy for me to figure out which.

In the morning our senses open up shop at staggered hours. Thus I suddenly heard, from beyond a window (and there, on schedule, my eyes once more slitting open, was the window in question), a cacophony of childlike whoops and squeals. I say suddenly, not because some children (in a park? in the playground of a nearby kindergarten?) had at that exact moment elected to start making merry, but because my hearing had just thrown open the shutters for the day ahead and these whoops and squeals were its first impatient customers. I shifted yet again and stretched my limbs to the bed's four corners, yawning with my whole body. Then I opened my eyes once and for all. Wan sunshine was seeping through the slats of olive-green shutters and dripping into the bedroom. The bedroom? On the wall to my right there hung a mirror in the shape of a giant teardrop. Under it was a black forged-iron table on which sat – alongside a lamp with a tangled-vine stem and a brass mesh shade in the form of a Crusader's visor – a two-headed Pompeiian vase, void of flowers. Next to that was a polished mahogany chest of drawers on top of which a Picassoish sculpture of an angular torso – who knows, perhaps it was even by Picasso –

sprawled like a large squashed insect. And, on the wall opposite me, there was the photograph, or Canalettograph, of the Venetian regatta.

I lay on, half in and out of sleep, mentally checking that everything was where it ought to be. Arms, legs, fingers, toes, abdomen, sexual organs – they were all there, present and correct. As the memories and modalities of dull diurnal consciousness chased away the florid efflorescences of my nocturnal double life – except that, during this last night, I realised with a pleasurable start, there had been no screech of tyres, no arch of snow-drenched trees, no lone snowman, no Ursula's face – my current spatial and temporal coordinates, as smartly drilled as a regiment of palace guardsmen, lined up in single file to await my inspection. First, I was in France, not England. *Tick.* Second, I had been released from the sanatorium. *Tick.* The Rolls-Royce. *Tick.* Béa. *Tick.* Sacha. *Tick.* The Georges de La Tour. *Tick.* Béa again, with whom I had gone to bed – the very first time I hadn't slept alone since Ursula's death. *Tick.* Then, in an unquantifiable rush, all the other facts and figures that made up the person I was. Yes, I said to myself, I now know all I need to know about my life as of today. I have the picture.

No one lay in bed at my side. A faint concavity suggestively puckered that half of the sheet on which Béa had slept but, as I discovered by shamelessly putting it to the test, there lingered no more intimate residue of her presence. She must have got up some time before.

I still had my wristwatch on. It was eight-twenty-two. I

rose, naked, and rubbed the butter pats from my eyes. On the floor beside the bed was a dressing-gown that I'd briefly worn the night before, while padding in and out of the bathroom. Intrigued to have at hand another example of Jean-Marc's taste, I picked it up and casually examined it. In silver and grey satin, it had a repeated motif of a pair of café-society fashion plates, a young man in lounge lizard frippery, patent leather pumps, soft black silk bowtie and starchy wing collar, and a young woman in a gossamer, ankle-length confection with a corsage of orchids, leaning over the deck rail of a 1930s ocean liner which, in the gown's second, diagonally alternating pattern, was also seen to be slicing through a stylised spray of prettily incurved foam. I slipped it over my shoulders, went to the window, poked a finger between a pair of slats and raised the upper slat like an epileptic's eyelid. There was no sign of the school or the park from which the whoops I'd heard might have emanated, but I noted that, although the sun was shining, it was obviously chilly, for the breath of passing cars was visible in the still unrisen mist. I also noted, striding alertly past the villa, a woman not much older than a schoolgirl, with shapely black-stockinged legs and a ponytail. She was incredibly slim – all waist – and wearing what I took at first to be earmuffs but which was actually a Walkman, or at any event some compact little gadget emitting sounds which, like Joan of Arc, only she could hear. Out front in the driveway was parked the Rolls.

Taking my time, more time than I was accustomed to

taking at home, I washed, cleaned my teeth with my forefinger, sleeked my hair back with saliva and wandered downstairs into the salon. No Béa. The curtains were open but nothing else had been tidied up, and the room, for all its airy elegance, had a bleary, morning-after feel to it. While I stood there puzzling whether I ought to call out Béa's name, I heard, from one of the adjoining rooms that I'd never entered, a queer sort of noise, as of some flustered scuffling or scrabbling at ground level. I walked across the salon, stood at the half-open door and looked in.

The room was a muskily scented library, dark and virile. Someone has been used to smoking a pipe here, I thought. Against a wall leaned a metal stepladder every one of whose steps was piled with books, so that a second, more elevated ladder, rising parallel to the first, seemed to be following in its footsteps. There were other books scattered about the floor and gaps in the wall shelving that they had once presumably filled. In one corner was a table with a chessboard top. In the opposite corner, supporting a jet-black television set as mirrory as its own screen, a stack of dusty bound volumes, each of them at a right angle to the one above and the one below, looked real enough from where I was standing but were most likely fake, carved from a single piece of painted wood. On the wall directly in front of me the lowest quarter of the wall shelving was not just hollow but open; on that shelving, too, the books were fakes. And rummaging inside the open section – rather, inside the safe which, as I could no longer doubt, it concealed, and which itself was concealed from my view by her own kneeling figure – was Béa. She hadn't heard me come in. Over her shoulder she was hurling buff envelopes and portfolios and bundles of papers knotted up in crimson ribbons. There was also, lying on a crescent-shaped rug that edged the hem of the divan like its gaudy Fauvist shadow, an album of Old Master drawings, carelessly thrown there, its sylphishly ethereal protective tissues cracked and torn.

'What are you looking for?'

My question caused Béa flickeringly to break off from what she was doing, but she didn't answer it.

'Béa, speak to me, what is it you're looking for?'

'Please don't interfere, Guy,' she said, without turning her head. 'It doesn't concern you.'

At that instant I understood what had gone missing and even how it had gone missing.

'It's "La Clé de Vair", isn't it?'

Nodding, she drew her right hand, empty, out from deep within the wall, fell back on the curled-up cups of her bare toes and pummelled her brow.

'Imbécile que je suis! Imbécile! Imbécile! Imbécile!'

'Sacha?'

She nodded again.

'Light me a cigarette, Guy, please. They're on the table in the salon.'

I returned to the salon, took two cigarettes from the ruby-red packet of Dunhills, lit them both and threaded one of them through her trembling fingers.

'When I rang him this morning, he slammed the phone down on me. Knowing Sacha, I shouldn't have been troubled by his antics, but I was, so I checked in the safe. He must have taken the painting with him when he stormed out last night. He's crazy, totally crazy. I never know what he's going to do.'

'Have you any idea where he might have gone?'

'He owns a studio along the coast, on Mont Saint-Michel. He doesn't actually live in it, you understand, it's where he goes to ground.' She let slip a last, hopeless bundle of papers on to the rug. 'I'll have to go there and try to reason with him. He'll listen to me, I think — I hope — but I really shouldn't delay, because Sacha is so highly-strung, he's liable to . . .'

She took my wrist and drew back the monkishly ample sleeve of Jean-Marc's dressing-gown to look at my watch.

'I'm sorry to be discourteous, Guy, but I'll have to borrow the Rolls back again, just for the trip. A morning at most.'

I shook my head.

'You won't give it to me?'

'I'm going with you.'

'Now that would be the very stupidest thing we could do. It was your presence that made him behave as he did in the first place. If he finds you with me . . .'

'I won't allow you to go alone. I don't trust Sacha and I'd rather not trust him there, at your side, than here alone. Don't forget, the car keys are still in my pocket. Like it or not, my darling,' I said, for once carrying off the kind of film-star nonchalance which has never come naturally to me, 'we're in this together.'

'If that's the case,' she said, without trying further to argue her case, 'you had better dress and shave. I want to leave in fifteen minutes.'

I took the driver's seat and eased the Rolls on to the vacant street. But just as I prepared to accelerate, a most extraordinary thing happened. From out of nowhere, with a brusqueness that had me jamming on the brakes, a youth stepped in front of the car. And what a youth! What I noticed about him first, through the car's by now none too pristine windscreen, was his hair. It had been cut in a Mohican style, each of its Struwwelpeter spikes greased and honed to a razor-like point. It was also multi-hued, running the gamut from chrome red through tea-rose pink to an Edenic green. The oddest thing of all was that this hairdo made him look as if he had a shaven head, as if the spikes were detachable from his cranium or had been artificially implanted on it. Except for his eyebrows, which overhung his eyes like two small symmetrical ridges on a cliffside, his face seemed concave rather than convex, but wilfully so, as if he were sucking in his features the way an overweight bather will suck in his paunch for as long as it takes him to tiptoe across the beach and immerse it in the ocean. As he started to approach the car, I saw that he was wearing a safety-pin on his right ear, that his black leather outfit was festooned with several other pins and that a string of razor-blades circled his neck. He stood at last, hands on hips, squarely in front of us.

Nonplussed, I lowered the window and would have stuck my head out had I not been prevented from doing so by another man who, having emerged out of the same nowhere as the first, was practically leaning on the Rolls. In every respect he couldn't have been less like his companion. At the skewed angle at which I had to look up at him, he appeared very tall; yet he was also, for so tall a man, unusually well-built. Beneath an unbuttoned black overcoat, he wore a dove-grey suit and waistcoat, as well as a tie of an irregular, black-and-white, eye-jazzing design. He was balding, and what was left of his creamy white hair had been whipped up over his ears to create the effect, an effect it was impossible to believe hadn't been intentional, of an eighteenth-century periwig. And he was smiling – or, should I say, there was a smile on his lips, which isn't after all the same thing.

'Good morning,' he said in an almost deferential tone, 'my name is Rieti. Mr Rieti. Shall we rearrange ourselves?'

Béa and I gaped at one another.

Rieti put his head through the window, so close to mine I could smell his breath.

'Don't worry, Madame Cheret. We shan't leave you behind. We mean to give both of you a lift.'

'A lift?' said Béa.

'A lift, yes, indeed. For I have the impression that we're all of us going in the same direction. Which direction that is, I confess I don't yet know, but I expect to find out by and by. Shall we make ourselves comfortable for the journey?'

'Look here,' I began, 'I don't know who –'

'No, of course you don't. But you will – oh, dear me, yes, you will.'

To the youth who was still blocking the road he called, 'Junior!'

As the latter slouched over to the car with a cowpoke's bandy gait, Rieti whispered to us both, in a giggle of an aside, 'I call them all Junior. Isn't he marvellous, though? The last of the Mohican cuts – that's my Junior.' And his frame shook with a booming laugh which seemed to jumble everything up inside his waistcoat.

Rieti and Junior were now standing on either side of the car. If I'd started the engine there and then, I'd probably have got away with it. But I was hypnotised by their strange music-hall double act and remained so while Rieti opened one door and Junior, at the same time, the other.

'Now, sir,' said Rieti to me, 'we're coming with you, whether you wish it to be so or not, so please let's have no phony heroics. If you would, but discreetly, discreetly, dear fellow, move into the back seat beside me, Junior will take over at the wheel. Madame Cheret, you will stay just where you are. I repeat, no rough stuff, please. Junior here' – this particular interjection was reserved for me alone – 'will snap your neck as easily as he would a breadstick. And though no hit man myself, heaven forfend, I do have upon my person a creaky but still highly efficient revolver' – he tapped his overcoat's right pocket, which was certainly bulging with something solid – 'and I'd be happy to take a potshot at, shall we say to start with, a pinkie or some nice fat thumb. Now, are we all ready to take our places?'

I glanced at Béa, who hastily nodded at me as if to say, 'Just do what he asks.'

Finding myself, as I got out of the Rolls, momentarily cheek-by-jowl with Rieti, I exploited the immunity of our enforced physical proximity to have a good long look at him. Bulbous, his face was not at all bland. It had a real, if fleshy, force, a real personality. It resembled the kind of face one might see in a gallery of portraits of the century's petrified luminaries of humanism, Shaw, Mann, Wells, Ortega y Gasset, Sibelius, with a perverse dash of Aleister Crowley – that was it, what Rieti resembled most was some illegitimate, unnatural progeny of Sibelius and Crowley.

Our eyes met. He smiled without parting his lips, like someone ashamed of his teeth. And after I'd slid across the seat cover in the back, he followed me in and slammed the door. In the meantime, Junior had taken my former seat in front, beside Béa, and was gleefully fingering the steering wheel's ribbed black rubber.

We sat for a few seconds, the Rolls at a standstill and none of us inside it saying a word. Then Rieti spoke up.

'Madame Cheret, I look to you for directions. No more suspense, if you don't mind. Where exactly are we bound?'

'Who are you?' said Béa, turning at last to face him.

'A fair question, dear lady,' he clucked, genteelly bowing

his head. 'I am, as you already know, Rieti. I am in the employ of a certain Mr Nasr – ah, I see that that name means something to both of you. Well, Mr Nasr was – now how shall I put this? – he was not altogether satisfied with the tale of the tree struck by lightning. A wonderful tale in its own right, to be sure, but, alas, not quite, no, most definitely not quite plausible. All the more so as Mr Lantern, the complete stranger, the innocent bystander, seems to have been spending a lot of his time in your company since that picturesque episode.'

Béa tried to interrupt him, but Rieti raised an arm to arrest her before she could open her mouth.

'Understand me,' he said. 'I have been in Saint-Malo since day one of the operation. Everything you two have done – done in public – I have been privy to. A rather squalid precaution on Mr Nasr's part, you might argue, but then he is terribly keen to take possession of the painting and, besides, I need hardly remind you that he has already invested a substantial sum of money in the project. I note, by the way, that my allusion to the existence of a painting has not, as it might well have, flummoxed our friend Lantern, so I can only suppose that my instincts were right and that he has been fully apprised of what is at stake. But where was I? Ah yes. Now even if the story was indeed corroborated by you, Madame Cheret, and your husband, each independently of the other, Mr Nasr was nevertheless unable to still a suspicion that all was not well and finally ordered me, along with Junior of course, to take a somewhat more active role in the proceedings. Yes, madame, there it is. The advance you have received is safe enough, but on the basis of my reports back to him Mr Nasr has had to come to the conclusion – can you blame him? – that you yourself, alas, are no longer to be trusted. The painting is clearly not in the Villa Lazarus. You will therefore tell me where it can be found and I'll arrange for it to be shipped across the Channel.

'So there it is,' he concluded without, even then, pausing for breath. 'Have I told you everything you wished to know?'

Béa took a cigarette from her bag and, before lighting it, gave it three or four brittle taps against the packet, something which – although in a funny way in character – I had never actually seen her do, and God knows I'd seen her light a lot of cigarettes. Since it suggested to me that she was playing for time, I decided to answer first.

'The picturesque little episode, as you call it, is true. I give you my word of honour.'

'Oh, my dear sir, with respect . . .' murmured Rieti. 'Words of honour, words of honour – I'm not about to place my confidence in a word of honour.'

'I tell you we're both innocent of what it is you suspect.'

'Innocent, you say, innocent? Don't you realise, Lantern, that for those of my profession it's the innocent who cannot be trusted. Crooks I trust. Villains I understand. They have their speciality, and, heaven bless them for it, they can be depended upon to stick to it. Embezzlers don't blackmail. Arsonists don't cheat on their income tax. Serial killers don't hold up tobacconists' shops. Ah, but the innocent, now. They are, by definition, capable of anything, and we can never know what it is they *are* capable of until it's too late. Oh Lord, protect me from the innocent' – here Rieti joined the tips of his fingers together as if he truly were supplicating the Almighty. 'There is – yes, yes, yes, I will personally vouch for it – a species, an extremely fragile species, I grant you, but a species all the same, of honour among thieves. I have yet to find much honour among you honest folk.'

A silence followed this tirade. Then, a half-smile crimping her upper lip, Béa said, 'Tell me, Rieti, is it something you *work at* – being larger-than-life, I mean?'

Rieti stared at her, and even Junior ceased his puerile fiddling with the dashboard and turned to hear his master's riposte.

But the latter's features relaxed almost at once, and out of his tiny, prissy mouth came that same gong-like laugh.

'By heaven, madame, you're a remarkable woman, that you are! Quite remarkable! If only we could have met under more convivial circumstances!' He sighed. 'Ah, but we are wasting time, mine if not yours. Where, I repeat, is "La Clé de Vair"? If it is inside your villa, which I have serious cause to doubt, give it me now and in a couple of weeks you will be richer than you have ever dreamed. If not, let us be off at once to where it is.'

Béa calmly went on smoking, using the cigarette – as, I now realised, she had always used her cigarettes – as a prop, as a hoary but custom-sanctioned piece of business that steadied her hand and gave her time to prepare herself for the delivery of her next line. Here, though, she seemed to me to be running a serious risk in play-acting, since I could not only see but actually feel Rieti losing patience with what was too obvious a feint, too blatant a falsity. I could feel, beside me on the back seat, the tensing up of his boneless obesity.

'Madame, you keep me waiting,' he said.

What Béa finally told him was some, not all, of the truth. She told him, first, that – 'I'm sorry to have to repeat myself' – but that the two cars genuinely had been exchanged on the road to Saint-Malo. That, as Rieti suspected, the La Tour was no longer in the villa's wall-safe. That, since they had both reckoned it would be more secure in his studio, it was Jean-Marc's partner Alexandre Liebermann, whose name Rieti must know as the greatest living expert on the work of Georges de La Tour, who now had guardianship of it. And that she herself and I – 'Oh, "Guy", is it?' Rieti interjected, '– better and better!' – had decided that very morning to fetch it back.

There was a silence, then Rieti shrugged his shoulders.

'Good, good. Oh, I do not say I believe your story – why should I? – but I'm willing to go along with it if for no other reason than that it brings us nicely up to date – and on condition, you understand, that the next stage prove no less satisfactory. Where is this Mr Liebermann's studio?'

'Ah, well, there you see,' said Béa, 'there's a problem.'

'A problem. Yes, I thought there might be.'

From the dashboard Béa yanked out a small black tray,

rammed her cigarette butt into its tiny trash heap and closed it again with a snap.

'The problem is Sacha.'

'Sacha? Who is Sacha?'

'Alexandre. It was Sacha who discovered the painting, but ever since he did he's been unhappy with the scheme. He's a basically honest person, you see. He's even spoken of taking the canvas to the authorities and giving himself up. I know *I* can persuade him not to, though. Frankly, he's in love with me.'

'Naturally he is. He's a man, isn't he.'

'But if I arrived on his doorstep with you and . . .' – she stammered, as if the name were too far-fetched to be said aloud – 'with you and Junior, well, it might be enough to push him over the edge. I really do believe that, for everybody's sakes, Guy and I should go alone.'

Rieti looked at her almost as if he were studying a painting in a gallery. He breathed actorishly; I waited for him to stifle a yawn, but he wasn't that unsubtle. When he spoke, though, it was in an even stagier drawl. I couldn't help noticing, even so, that he had dispensed with the booming laugh.

'So. You claim you left the La Tour – for safekeeping, mind you – with an individual who, you also inform me, is "basically honest", an individual who even speaks of "giving himself up" to the police. This is unworthy of you, madame. Imagination, of which you have undoubted oodles, is nothing if it does not entail empathy with the needs and motivations of your fellow beings. One such need is not to have one's intelligence insulted. I don't pretend to understand the nature of the little game you are playing with my present needs and motivations, and I don't care if I never understand it. The money involved is not mine and, to be absolutely candid, and I do like a man to be candid whatever the circumstances, I personally don't give two hoots for Georges de La Tour. But I asked you a sensible question and I was offended by your reply. I was offended that I was taken for an idiot.'

'I certainly don't think you're an idiot.'

'No? Then let us have no more nonsense. Where, I repeat, is "La Clé de Vair"?'

'For the reason I gave you, Rieti, I can't –'

She never completed what it was she was about to say. With no fuss, absolutely no ado, Rieti pulled the revolver from his overcoat pocket and leaned forward in his seat. He took hold, from behind, of the shyly sloping neckline of Béa's blouse and stuck the barrel so far down her bare back only the fist that held it remained visible. Tickled by the scrape of cold metal on her naked skin, Béa's back stiffened up, her shoulder-blades suddenly tangible under the blouse's filmy veil. I started to make a move, but without looking at me Rieti said, 'Stay where you are, Lantern. Or I will surely pull the trigger.'

I had to hand it to him. So economically had the little coup been carried out, it was only on hearing Rieti's threat that Junior turned his head to catch up with what was taking place in the rest of the car.

Now, leaning further forward, and drawing aside, with a repulsively dainty gesture, one of her pearl-drop earrings, as if it might prevent her from hearing clearly what he had to say next, Rieti started whispering in Béa's ear.

'Listen to me, dear lady. I have twice put a simple question to you and I have twice been rebuffed. I'm a patient man – unlike many in my profession, I might add. So I will ask you a third and final time. But if you insist on stringing me along, I will pull the trigger, I swear it. I cannot be sure where the bullet will go. It might rip your delicate back open. It might lodge in the cleft of your no doubt equally delicate buttocks. Then again, it might miss your body altogether. That's a chance I'm prepared to take. It's a chance you must be prepared to take if you refuse to answer.'

'Béa, please!' I cried. 'For God's sake –'

'Mont Saint-Michel,' said Béa.

'Mont Saint-Michel?' Without removing his revolver, Rieti gave this new factor in the equation a whirl about his brain like a wine fancier complacently swilling a vintage Burgundy on his tongue. 'Mont Saint-Michel. How amusing. Where on Mont Saint-Michel?'

'Where?'

'What street? What street number?'

'I honestly don't know. Does Mont Saint-Michel have street numbers?'

'I warn you, madame, stop fooling with me,' said Rieti

with a frown. 'I'm uncorking my revolver' – he corrected himself with ponderous coyness – 'I am un*cock*ing my revolver – forgive the pun, the homespun pun – quite unintentional, I assure you.' This incongruous intrusion of joviality notwithstanding, he did uncock the revolver. I heard its click under the flimsy screen of Béa's blouse.

'Well, but wait, will you,' she said quickly. 'I really don't know the name of the street. Or the number. But I do know where Sacha's studio is. I'll recognise the house when I get there. Believe me, I'm telling you the truth.' And she repeated, 'Believe me.'

For about ten seconds Rieti paused. At last, with a leisurely deliberation which I, possibly too generously, ascribed to caution rather than cruelty, he withdrew the gun from inside Béa's blouse and replaced it in his overcoat pocket.

'Very well, madame,' he said, 'I fancy I do believe you. Or, let's say, I choose to believe you for the time being. Mont Saint-Michel it is.'

Sitting back comfily, he repeated, 'Mont Saint-Michel. How unexpectedly whimsical. And perhaps,' he added after a moment, 'perhaps once this needlessly messy business of ours has been concluded to all our respective satisfactions, we might, the four of us, sup at La Mère Poularde. It is, I've been told, *the* restaurant of Mont Saint-Michel. Sir Winston Churchill once dined there, and the Pompidous – or does one say "Pompidoux" with an *x*? No matter.'

He rubbed his large, pancakey palms together. 'Now,' he

said expansively, 'now that our *mauvais quart d'heure* is at an end, why don't we all settle down and try to enjoy the little excursion that lies ahead of us? What, I wonder, does *notre cher* Proust have to say on the matter?'

From the other, revolverless pocket of his overcoat, which bulged hardly less than its mate, he extracted a frayed paperback, curling at the edges, of what, it transpired, was *Sodom and Gomorrah*, the fourth volume, at least in its English translation, of Proust's *A la recherche du temps perdu*. To my astonishment, he opened it at random, let his eyes roam for a few seconds over a double spread of pages, then started to read: '*If the act of going out to dinner, to which I had grown so indifferent, by taking the form, which entirely revivified it, of a journey along the coast followed by an ascent in a carriage to a point six hundred feet above the sea, had produced in me a sort of intoxication, this feeling had not been dispelled at La Raspelière.*'

A silence. Then he closed the volume as reverently as if to say, 'What *can* I say?' Even had I cared to offer an opinion, I doubtless would not have been allowed to, for there was a despotic nuance to Rieti's wonderment that also appeared to be telling us: no, no, don't speak, not yet, don't break the spell of the miracle to which we have just been witness.

It was he himself who finally did.

'How apt, how awesomely apt! Ah, but that's Proust for you. This novel', he said, tapping its dog-eared cover with his index finger, 'is not just one literary masterpiece among others, it is *all* of literature. Read Proust and you will never have to read anything else. For the past twenty-seven years I haven't found the need to open another book. I start at the beginning of *Swann's Way* and, when I reach the end of *Time Regained*, why, I start all over again. And if ever I should find myself in a crisis – or, as now, happily, if ever the storm clouds of crisis have just dissipated – I open whatever volume it is I chance to be reading at the time and I have never, *never*, failed to hit on a sentence which did not strike at the heart of the matter at hand. Proust, in a word, is my Bible.'

I couldn't believe it. Here I was, in Saint-Malo, held prisoner – inside a Rolls-Royce that was not my own – by a grotesque gangster and his punkish gunsel, hair radiating from his skull like a golden sunburst mirror above a mantelpiece. And now here he was, the gangster himself, spouting Proust at me. It was a joke, it was a horrible joke.

Rieti himself, however, was all bustling ebullience again.

'Let us be off out of this unutterably dismal little town. Madame Cheret, you will please give Junior the directions he requires. As I recall, Mont Saint-Michel is but an hour or so along the coastal road as the Einsteinian crow flies – "*along the coast followed by an ascent to a point six hundred feet above the sea*", awesome, simply awesome! – and the most urgent question facing us now is how we get on to that road. I leave it up to you.'

With these words, he pulled a fat cigar from an inside pocket of his overcoat. He unwrapped it, savagely bit off its tip and spat the disgusting driblet out of the half-open window. He lit the cigar, inhaling then slowly exhaling, and I watched, enthralled, as a superb smoke ring hovered for an instant in the back of the low-ceilinged car, exactly halfway between the two of us, like a halo without a saint, until it disintegrated before our eyes.

Fifteen minutes later we had escaped from Saint-Malo and were at last on the road along which Béa and I had already driven the previous night. Beneath us the ocean heaved, each of the successive creases on its wavy surface ironed out, as it approached the shoreline, by a rolling cylinder of spume that would then decompose on the beach, spreading a dark arc of soaking wetness across the sand like an egg white cracked into a sizzling frying pan. Above us was high, windswept meadowland with only an infrequent farmhouse to break the monotony; that and some riotously barking dog that would hurl itself against the farmhouse gate as we drove by. The sun had been eclipsed. Low, pendulous clouds, cold and unpromising, gloomed the Rolls's windscreen, and I could tell there was a salty wind abroad and even glimpsed, on the horizon, a sodden rainbow whose colours had sloppily begun to run.

In the driver's seat in front of me, Junior said nothing. Except when he overtook another car and let out a guttural 'Va va va voom!', as if the Rolls were vacuuming up huge, heart-rending distances instead of proceeding along the northwestern coastline of France at a speed respectful of every prevailing limit, I hadn't yet heard the sound of his voice. I observed, though, that every so often he would steal a lascivious glance at Béa and then fidget in his seat, endeavouring to find the most comfortable position for all his intimate chattels. She, meanwhile, stubbed cigarette after cigarette into the dashboard ashtray, holding each one down hard until the last wisp of smoke, the very last breath of life, had been extinguished from it, like someone drowning a kitten in a stream.

All of which suggests that we were motoring in silence. Not so. Rieti, a chatterbox, kept up a jovial running commentary – on Béa's delusion that she would have been able to keep the truth from him, on the story of the lightning-struck tree ('Wonderful, wonderful, I did so enjoy hearing it'), on what would happen to us were there any further misjudgments on our part and on anything else that happened to catch his fancy. And then there was Proust. It was revealed, for instance, that Rieti actually lived in Nasr's mansion in Kent and, when he began to expatiate on the joys of living in the country instead of in the city, he burbled, 'Oh, but I know the divine Marcel could put it so much better than I. Let us see, let us see.' And he fetched out the copy of *Sodom and Gomorrah*, opened it at any old page, so it seemed, and read: ' "*Then the rays of the sun gave place suddenly to those of the rain; they streaked the whole horizon, enclosing the line of apple-trees in their grey net.*" Exquisite, simply exquisite,' he sighed, smacking his lips like someone who has just eaten a peach, or an apple from one of Proust's trees, and quietly giving himself up to internal musings on the sentence's analogical aptitude. Then, ten minutes later, when we passed a cluster of melancholy mountain goats perched on different levels of the hillside like the chorus of an old-fashioned opera production (that, I admit, was Rieti's simile, not mine), out came Proust again, browsed at random, recited with hammy orotundity: ' "*The horses of sleep, like those of the sun, move at so steady a pace, in an atmosphere in which there is no longer any resistance, that it requires some little meteorite extraneous to ourselves (hurled from the azure by what Unknown?)*" – "*hurled from the azure by what Unknown?*" ' he repeated, shaking his heavy head as if disbelieving of the conceit's suitability and splendour – ' "*to strike our regular sleep (which otherwise would have no reason to stop, and would continue with a similar motion world without end) and to make it swing sharply round, return towards reality, travel without pause, traverse the regions bordering on life*" – "*traverse the regions bordering on life*", by God, sir, he's incredible! – "*whose sounds the sleeper will presently hear, still vague but already perceptible even if distorted – and come to earth suddenly at the point of awakening.*"

'I ask you, Lantern,' he said to me after a long reflective pause, 'could it be better put? I mean to say, assuming that is what you wanted to say, could it be better said? Sir, I insist not.'

'But,' I ventured, '– the relevance? I don't see the relevance.'

Rieti snorted. 'My dear Lantern – and you a writer!'

'Not that kind of a writer, I'm afraid,' I replied.

But I was wasting my breath. His eyes swimming, he continued: '*Remembrance of Things Past* is a sacred text, and that is how it must be read – not as one reads a book but as one might read the world. The relevance escapes you at this moment, perhaps, but one day, I swear, it will strike you as suddenly as – ah, as a bolt of lightning!' – and once more I had the impression that the inside of his waistcoat contained all manner of objects, frying pans, fobwatches, compasses, footwarmers, God knew what else, to be given a good jumbling up whenever he shook with laughter – 'and then you will realise that Proust is not for the trice, the wink, the indifferent blink.'

He fell silent. Settling himself well back in the seat, he even closed his eyes, the better to reflect, I supposed, on the infinitude of Proustian arcana. The paperback of *Sodom and Gomorrah* lay spread open on his lap, face down in the form of a giant circumflex. My view of the road ahead was blocked by Junior's spikes. Against my thigh I could feel, in Rieti's coat pocket, the intimidating solidity of his revolver.

And it was then the realisation came to me that if I were ever to do something about our situation it was now that the thing would have to be done. I was an averagely brave but also averagely cowardly man, whose sole previous exposure to the proposition that a human destiny could be determined by a single, impulsive act had been in the cinema – and, even there, it had never been the kind of film I preferred. Yet because the moment I was living through actually did recall some scene from a film I'd seen – a Hitchcock? – I told myself that the initiative was mine if only I had the nerve to take it.

Easing my left hand – I didn't dare use my right – out of

the narrow gap formed by my hip and the window of the Rolls, I let it sidle across my knees. Slowly, very slowly, I groped the broad, woolly flap of the coat pocket beside me. Nothing. Not a sound, not a stirring from Rieti. I waited for about twenty seconds, then stealthily raised the flap and inserted my hand inside. Still nothing. I felt the tips of my fingers brush against the barrel of the revolver and I was just about to grasp its handle – when Rieti's eyes opened. For an instant nothing happened. I didn't move, I didn't even attempt to withdraw my hand. Bemused, as if hardly bothered, Rieti gazed down at the flap and at the arm that led from it like a flex. Suddenly, before I had time to react, he caught my wrist in his own hand and pressed his thumbnail deep into the vein of my pulse until a globule of blood squirted out of it. I yelped. I momentarily looked away from my tormentor to meet Béa's eyes with my own. At the very moment I did, my head exploded. A lonely snowman began to melt in slow motion, floating upward, upward, ever upward, sprinkling the air with snow-sparks, before turning into an enormous soapy-white bubble of nothingness.

I don't know how long I was out. When I came to, I nearly burst into tears, so acute was the pain searing the back of my head. The first thing I heard was Rieti's voice, but distant and indistinct, as if he were talking through the wrong end of a megaphone and it was having the same effect on his speech as looking through the wrong end of a telescope would have had on his vision. What he was saying was fractious, shredded – bitter, disconnected phrases and half-phrases in search of a sentence structure. I heard '. . . utterly foolish . . . it certainly doesn't inspire . . . something I ought . . . tell me honestly, madame . . .'

I heard Béa answer him, coldly and metallically, but I couldn't make out at all what *she* was saying, for at that point she still had her back to me and was talking to the windscreen. The interior of the car was suffused with the blended stench of cigar and cigarette smoke. Béa turned round to face me with eyes clouded by love and fear. I dragged my head up to the window. On the choppy surface of the sea two small white-sailed yachts were rising and dipping out of sight, rising and dipping again, battered so mercilessly by foam-flecked rollers they were most of the time flat on their sides like a pair of kites that had come down, smack, in the Atlantic. The car's voices rasping in my ears, I watched those two yachts for a few seconds. Then I saw, some way beyond them, a rocky black protuberance, no more than a dozen yards square, less like an island than a lump of seabed that the ocean had failed to submerge. As an element of scenery, it was completely without interest, and there could well have been, on the road between Saint-Malo and Mont Saint-Michel, a number of others similar and even identical to it to which I had paid no attention. But, for as long as the Rolls's window remained aligned with its stout yet tapering form, I found myself troubled by some inexplicably anxiety-inducing hint of meaningfulness whose source as yet, in my stunned condition, I was incapable of locating. I stared and stared at it – it was almost as if, almost as if – but no, the Rolls was already moving on and carrying off the meaning with it. Except that, when we and the island had finally gone our separate ways, we forward, it backward, and it had vanished from the window frame, its bleached-out after-image clung on for the longest time to the lining of my brain.

It dissolved only when I heard Rieti address me.

'Well, sir, are you pleased with yourself?'

'Pleased with myself?' I said; and, wincing, immediately had to pull my eyebrows down over eyes that were misting with pain.

'Your absurd derring-do has done nothing but give you an atrocious headache and, I should add, made it that little bit harder for me – not, mark you, that it was ever easy – to believe what you and madame have been telling me. Let's have no more such antics.'

As he spoke, he kept fondling his revolver, and I realised that it was with it that he had beaned me. After a while, putting it away, he fussily tweaked his coat-buttons and brushed specks of imaginary dandruff from his shoulders. Then he fished out *Sodom and Gomorrah*, buried himself in the labyrinth of its serpentine sentences, its subordinate clauses seemingly attached by safety-pins, and said not another word.

Fifteen minutes elapsed. The coastal road unwound before us. Béa and I exchanged glances but didn't speak. Junior

drove on as before, now without any 'Va va va voom!'
noises.

Suddenly, Béa turned to him and, her voice hardly raised
above a whisper, enquired if he had a spare cigarette. I could
see his neck redden as he took a flattened packet of
Marlboros from one of the pockets of his black leather jacket.
Rieti raised a curious eye, but at once returned to his
reading. Béa lit the cigarette, exhaled and, still more or less in
a whisper, asked Junior how old he was.

'Twenty-two,' he said, with a drawl that sounded not so
much American as an English disc jockey's hopeful go at
passing for American. Removing his hand from the steering
wheel, he tweaked the slickest of the stalks that stood up on
his skull.

'Garbo talks,' said Béa.

'S'right,' he mumbled with a foxy grin.

'You know,' she said to him, 'it's a shame you've
encumbered yourself with all that punkish paraphernalia.
You're a good-looking boy. You have beautiful teeth, a nice
friendly smile, lovely – now what colour are they?' (she
leaned sideways to peer into his inflamed face) – 'lovely
brown eyes. I wish we could see you as you really are under
the camouflage.'

Junior blushed outright. Rieti glanced up from his Proust.
Head cocked, he looked at Béa in some puzzlement.

'How nice of you to say so, my dear Madame Cheret,' he
eventually said. 'On this matter at least you and I see eye to
eye. It's long been my fondest wish to get the boy into more

fetching apparel. Nothing too formal, you understand – no blazers, no flannels, nothing with silver buttons and buckles. Some stylish casual wear, I fancy. He would look delightful in a polo shirt and a pair of designer jeans.'

Junior grunted, amiably enough, 'Can it, will you.'

Letting his two eyes rise heavenward, Rieti sighed. 'Wasn't it Emerson who said that no spiritual satisfaction could ever match the physical well-being of a perfectly fitting set of clothes?'

To which Junior, with a sidelong look at Béa, and displaying a hitherto unsuspected gift for knowing just how to prick his master's pomposity, replied, 'It sure sounds like one of his.'

Rieti caught that sidelong look, and his mouth tightened at the corners.

'I wouldn't like you to turn his head,' he said to Béa. 'He's used to receiving compliments only from me.'

'You make him sound like a well-trained Labrador.'

'Fie, fie, madame.'

Béa turned again to the boy.

'And you, Junior. Don't you have anything to say for yourself?'

'Me?' he answered incredulously, as if no one had ever invited him to speak his piece before.

'Yes, you. Tell us something about yourself.'

If it had been possible, which his hair made it not, I had the feeling that Junior would have scratched his head like a yokel in a barnyard farce.

'I can tell a joke,' he said hesitantly.

'Yes, please. Let's have a joke.'

'Madame Cheret,' said a languid Rieti beside me, 'I do not advise it. Really not. Junior's jokes are usually unfit for mixed company.'

'Don't be so stuffy. I've heard dirty jokes before. Tell us your joke, Junior,' she said, bending almost amorously towards him.

'Well, this one isn't really dirty.'

'No need to apologise,' said Béa. 'I quite like the other kind too.'

'Well, okay,' said Junior, and he cleared his throat. 'So – so these two limousines meet in the middle of a bridge and it's too narrow, see, for both of them to pass at the same time. So they pull up opposite each other and the – the two drivers – uh, what do you call them? – the chauffeurs – the two chauffeurs get out of their limousines and walk to the middle of the bridge. And the first chauffeur says to the second chauffeur, "You know, old chap" – this is in England, right? Did I say this was all happening in England?'

'Oh, for God's sake, get on with it,' snapped Rieti.

'Now, now,' said Béa, 'you'll put him off. Go on, Junior. Take your own time.'

'Yeah, well, this is all taking place in England. Okay, so the first chauffeur says, "You know, old chap, sorry, but you're going to have to back up." And the second chauffeur – he just looks at him like and he says, "Oh yeah? So why've I got to be the one that backs up?" And the first chauffeur says, "You got any idea who I got in that limo?" And the second chauffeur says, "No. Who?" And the first chauffeur says, "Lady Diana, that's who." So then the first chauffeur – no, the second chauffeur – the second chauffeur says, "Is that right? Lady Diana, you don't say –" '

Something abruptly arrived to distract the telling of the joke – an enormous articulated truck which, from the opposite direction, had crept up on us unseen behind a tufty cliff protruding right on to the road. It was a mild enough swerve that Junior had to make to avoid it, one any competent driver would have known how to manoeuvre without a qualm, but I could hear Rieti all but gnashing his teeth. Junior, though, paid no heed to the growing rumble of disapproval from his back.

'So then he says, "Well, you just come with me, my good man," and he takes the – the – the first chauffeur back to *his* limo and he opens the door and there, sitting inside, is the Queen, the Queen of England, okay? And the – the *second* chauffeur points at the Queen – who's just sitting there, see, just minding her own business – and he says to the first chauffeur, "So what do you think this is, a piece of shit?" '

There was a long pause. Although Junior's eyes were doggishly begging her to get the joke, for a second or two Béa offered no reaction at all. Then, all at once, she laughed out loud, laughed with, to my ears, a forced and rather tinkly 'ha ha ha' that sounded as if each 'ha' were tripping down a sunlit flight of stepping stones.

Rieti looked at her coldly.

'You astonish me, madame. I hardly expected in you such tolerance for low, vulgar, tribal humour.'

'Why, Monsieur Rieti,' said Béa with a mischievous smile. 'Don't tell me you never laughed at something in your day, something you knew was idiotic, something that made you laugh just because it was idiotic.'

'No, I didn't. And I'll have you know, madame, this *is* my day.'

'Well, I found it very funny,' said Béa. 'And Junior knew it was idiotic when he told it to us. Didn't you?'

'Uh. Yeah, sure,' said Junior dubiously.

'There, you see,' said Béa to Rieti. 'You keep him on too tight a leash. He may have gifts of which you know nothing.'

'I think not, madame. Junior is a sweet, artless boy. When I'm with him, I feel as if I've had a complete change of blood. And I don't care for you or anybody else to be putting ideas into his head. Is that quite clear?'

'I assure you it was not my intention. And I promise never to put ideas into his head again. What is it you British say – cross my heart and hope to die?'

'Let us hope *not*, shall we?' said Rieti. Then, inevitably, 'Proust, I know, will be his unfailingly apt and unerring self.' He riffled through the volume before flicking it open and reading the following paragraph: '*As for the sculptor Ski – so styled on account of the difficulty they found in pronouncing his Polish surname, and because he himself, since he had begun to move in a certain sphere, affected not to wish to be associated with his perfectly respectable but slightly boring and very numerous relations –*

he had, at forty-five and distinctly ugly, a sort of boyishness, a dreamy wistfulness which was the result of his having been, until the age of ten, the most ravishing child prodigy imaginable, the darling of all the ladies.'

He sat back.

'Ah yes. A bit oblique, a bit circuitous, but saying what it means to say, nevertheless. Amazing, is it not?'

Béa said nothing. Instead, and almost as if she hadn't heard him speak, she continued to direct her attention exclusively at poor Junior.

'How do you feel about all of this?' she asked him. 'How do you like people thinking of you as his little, his little – wifie?'

Before Junior could reply, Rieti interceded.

'Do be judicious, Madame Cheret. I recommend you not to do or say anything that you will live to regret – that you *won't* live to regret.' He tilted forward and placed a hand on the boy's shoulder. 'Junior, my dear, I hope it's as obvious to you as it is to me what this pest of a woman, this nonpareil pain in the butt, is endeavouring to do. Hers is the oldest trick in what is already the oldest and wormiest of books. Do, please, justify my faith in you by not rising to so very maggoty a bait.'

Junior, however, having offered no answer to this, and Rieti himself clearly preferring not to aggravate what he must have been aware was a dangerously sensitive truce, he then fell back into a cagey silence. I sat just as silently beside him, my head still painful to the touch, and turned to look out of the window. On the windswept beach beyond the rocks I saw an elderly man in a sheepskin-lined coat, his flannel trousers rolled up to his knees, paddling his bare feet in the icy shallows. Standing a few yards away from him, on the sand, an adolescent in jeans and wellington boots, probably his grandson, was having fun making a succession of smooth, flat pebbles play leap-frog with the ocean, until each in turn wearily subsided into the cool serenity of its depths. Beyond them both lay the open sea, and the mazy blue knots which its swell everlastingly ravelled and unravelled, and the pale ridges of foam which curled and uncurled on the crest of each succeeding wave, as if the breeze were turning the pages of some vast maritime log-book. It was an image of nature and normality that forcibly brought home to me, as if I needed to have it brought home to me, how far along the road I had already travelled from both.

The moment passed and I came to myself again. As I did, Junior, his left hand on the steering wheel, was turning to Béa and saying with a lickerish leer, 'I'm nobody's little wifie, but I'd be happy to be your little hubby – if you think you can handle a *real* man.'

Although taken aback, she smiled. Whereupon, lighting one of her eternal Dunhills, she exhaled a thin jet of smoke straight at the windscreen, against which it silently splattered.

'Well, well,' she said. 'If I'm any judge of these things, which I am, you aren't the type who wastes much time.'

Rieti paled. He stooped forward, groping inside his coat pocket. With a sharp tug that caused his elbow unpleasantly to prod mine, he found what he was looking for, and at once the revolver was sitting on his lap again.

Junior, meanwhile, was treating Béa to what he must have believed was a look of confident sassiness, a look in which, at any rate, was expressed all the cocky insolence of youthful maleness.

'And if I'm any judge,' he said, 'which I am, neither are you.'

Béa's half-amused and half-horrified gaze suddenly dropped to his lap, and without actually seeing anything of what was going on I instantly knew that, with his free hand, he had obscenely plumped up his crotch like a pillow.

'So . . . so that's something you and I have in common,' she said. Then, with slow, sly deliberation, 'But, you know, Junior, it's what we *don't* have in common that interests me.' And, letting her body swayingly encroach on his half-share of the Rolls's front seat, she scooped up the whole kit and caboodle of his crotch in her right hand and, as hard as she could, dug her long, laquered fingernails into its fleshy tenderness.

Even before he screamed, Junior's bald neck flared up as if consumed by flames from the inside, reminding me, for the very first time in a long time, of the plane tree which had been struck by lightning. At the same time, removing both hands from the steering wheel to minister to his martyred privates, he let his head fall back hard against the seat, and I observed that, although his eyes were shut, tears were spurting out over their lashes.

So much seemed to happen at once. When Junior had thrown his head backward, his legs were clamped tight together. An instant later, with a shudder that had the effect of making his whole body go rigid, they sprang wide open again, lewdly wide, and his right leg jammed up against the wheel, propelling it furiously rightward. Fortunately, there was no traffic heading our way, but the Rolls careened off its prescribed lane in the three-lane road and started heading straight for the barbed-wire fence and the sunken ditch that had accompanied us since we quit Saint-Malo.

With unexpected presence of mind, Béa rapidly bent across the now prone Junior, who was cradling his smarting crotch to a doleful lullaby of moans, his half-open eyes runnily bloodshot, and jerked the untended steering wheel to the left, with such force that she sent us all flying sideways while the Rolls abruptly shot across the road again towards the clifftop and the drop and the ocean beneath. Rieti and I shouted out simultaneously. And, no more than a couple of seconds after distractedly withdrawing her hand from the wheel, she grasped it once more and started to pull it in the opposite direction, endlessly turning it and turning it and turning it as if struggling to open up or close down some great valve in a rusting dam. Blanching, Rieti did the absolutely worst thing he could have done. He looked out of the window at the hole in space and the slimily glittering rocks which formed a scaly black pie-crust on the beach hundreds of feet below us and, in his shock, he let slip his revolver, which slid across the floor of the car before coming to a halt at my feet, revolving on its intoxicated axis like a coin spun on a bar counter. He looked to be on the point of throwing up, and I really think he would have done had not Béa's mighty exertions with the steering wheel belatedly taken effect. Like the sort of roller-coaster which, to its gaily petrified passengers, appears about to take off into space and changes its mind only at the last possible moment, the Rolls lurched yet again and began to make its drunkenly erratic way back to the other side of the road. Nothing could stop it now. It sliced through the barbed-wire fence and stopped short, with a brain-rattling bump, on the very edge of the ditch.

Perhaps because I had already received a numbing blow to my system, a blow from which I had still not recovered, I bore the brunt of the shock better than the others. Rieti had been bounced forward by the jolt and sat, parchment-pale, a tricklet of blood seeping out from one of his nostrils, his forehead glued to the seat in front of him. Junior had been hurled – more likely, had had the quick wits to thrust himself – back, not forward, at the instant of impact. Greedily gulping in vast quanta of air, he continued to clutch the steering wheel in his two hands, if now at a queerly rigid arm's length. Béa was seated bolt upright. I noticed to my dismay what I at first thought must be a puddle of blood on her lap, but it turned out to be the packet of Dunhill cigarettes which, along with an anonymous assortment of keys, had clattered out of the glove compartment.

She was shaking when I touched her on the shoulder.

'Béa, are you hurt?'

She shook her head, glanced back at Rieti, then at poor Junior, whose day this was most definitely not, and said, 'No . . . No, not too badly.'

'Are you sure?'

'Yes, yes, I'm fine. Let's get the hell out of here!'

'Where are we to go? And what should we do about them?'

'Fuck them. This is our only chance. Are you able to open the door on your side?'

After a dozen vain efforts, when its handle would connect with nothing and just flopped limply and sweatily under the pressure of my arm like the lever of a stranger's lavatory that embarrassingly refuses to be flushed, I eventually succeeded in opening the door. As I squeezed myself out, one of my shoes tapped against a hard object and I realised at once that it was Rieti's revolver. It's true that, in my haste to escape from the car, I had accidentally kicked it away from me under the seat so that it would have been an onerous and time-wasting business retrieving it. Retrieve it, though, I certainly could have done; and I knew too that, were I to have mentioned the fact to Béa, she would have insisted that we take it and at once turn the tables on Rieti. Why, then, did I leave it behind? I realise now that the end of our adventure might have – no, *would* have – been very different if I had secured it for Béa and myself. But there you are – perhaps, I tell myself, because I was still more alarmed by the idea of such a weapon in Béa's hands than in Rieti's – I didn't. I left it where it was.

She and I got out of the car at the same moment. Her skirt, I noticed, was speckled with blood, while the hem of my jacket's inside pocket had been ripped open when we took our nosedive and its contents – a fountain pen, a comb, a leather portable diary whose hollow spine snugly sheathed a tiny gold pencil – now lay scattered over the floor. Both of us had landed with our feet in the ditch, but were otherwise unharmed. Behind us, inside the Rolls, neither Rieti nor Junior stirred, and even the latter's moaning had ebbed away.

I took Béa's hand in mine and with her started to climb the mossy, stony, surprisingly steeply raked slope which led upward, as I trusted, to some plateau of regular, unbroken greenery high above the coastal road. Still shaken up from the accident, we stubbed our toes against weedy outgrowths of rock and scuffed our waterlogged shoes on small sandy inclinations and dislodged little communities of pebbles that then went cascading down the hillside. The slope grew ever steeper as we rose, hillocks materialising behind other hillocks, and it was soon made clear to me that my vague appraisement of its altitude from the level of the road had been much too optimistic. But just as I was beginning to wonder if we'd ever reach the top, a solitary guinea fowl, as if sprung from a trap, soared up with an earsplitting squawk, the open sky hove into sight and we had arrived.

I peeled back my shirt-cuff to consult my wristwatch. It

was one minute short of half-past-two. Far below us, at the side of a bizarrely askew Rolls, were Rieti and Junior – the latter still hopping from one foot to another, his hands clamped over his crotch. Ahead of us was a narrow glade of trees, no more than four or five rows of them. And, a dozen yards beyond that, there was what looked like an indefinite stretch of flat meadowland, one that would take us who knew where but at least out of reach of our pursuers. I silently indicated its existence to Béa.

Hand in hand, half walking, half running, we made our way through the glade. Springy, dry, bone-brittle twigs crackled under our feet. A stray branch of a tree, pushed aside by Béa without a second thought, bounced backward and whipped me across the chest. The grid of light and shade dappling the treetops above our heads seemed to give prominence first to light, then to shade, making it impossible to tell which of the two constituted the basis, the 'ground', of its dovetailing interplay. During the few minutes that our crossing lasted, too, I had the sense of a host of omnipresent little creatures vigilantly biding their time inside their lairs until we galumphing humans had vacated their territory.

On the far side of the glade, bordered by another barbed-wire fence, the grass turned out to be not only greener but also, contrary to all our expectations, as lush and even as that of an English lawn. About a hundred yards away glinted the surface ripple of a small pond in front of which an oak fanned its gigantic green tail against the sky like a peacock. Clasping

Béa's hand, I started to run towards its leafy overhang, where we'd be able to get our breath back before continuing.

We sat against the trunk, side by side, our bodies heaving. Finally, I turned to face her.

'Béa, there's something I don't understand.'

'What?'

'Why – well, why are we here at all?'

She stared at me in incomprehension.

'Why are we here?' She laughed harshly. 'What a question to ask now!'

'Look – Rieti's a bastard, agreed. But, after all, he *is* the agent of – what was his name again? – Nasr? He *is* the man you're supposed to be selling the painting to, isn't he?'

'You know he is.'

'So why on earth are we running away from him?'

There was no response from Béa.

'It just doesn't make sense.'

She still didn't speak.

'I mean, was it really necessary to crash the car and put our lives at risk? Anything could have happened.'

Silence.

'Oh, for Christ's sake, say something, will you!'

She took my hand and carefully folded her own over and under it.

'Guy, have you forgotten Rieti already? Forgotten that gun of his? How he abused me with it? And knocked you out? And his voice! If I'd had to listen to another word from that pompous windbag, I swear –' and the pitch of her own voice started to rise until I thought it was going to crack.

'No, Béa, I haven't forgotten,' I said. 'What I don't understand, though, is how we could ever have got ourselves into such an incredible scrape. You want to sell the La Tour, Rieti wants to buy it. So where's the problem?'

'The problem? Sacha is the problem. I couldn't possibly let those two goons follow us to Mont Saint-Michel. You've already had a sample of Sacha's behaviour. What do you suppose he'd do now if they were to come barging into his studio?'

'Yes, yes, I know, but it's still a mystery to me –'

The sentence, however, was left hanging. Something, invisible but audible enough, had just pinged past us. Without thinking, I leapt to the ground and dragged Béa with me.

For a couple of seconds we lay there together, face down, panting in unison.

Then Béa whispered to me, 'Guy, what's happening?'

'Surely you felt it?' I said.

'Felt what?'

'The bullet. You must have felt it. It only just missed us.'

'No. No, I felt nothing.'

After a moment, keeping herself out of sight behind the tree, she peered around its trunk in the direction of the glade, the cliff and, beyond them, the ocean's no longer visible hem.

'I can't see either Rieti or Junior.'

'They must be there somewhere.'

She sat back beside me, pulling her knees up to her chin like a drawbridge over a castle moat.

'I can only imagine,' she whispered, 'that this little show of theirs is designed to scare us. But since what Rieti wants is the La Tour, he can't kill us and he knows it.'

I inwardly cursed myself for not having after all retrieved Rieti's revolver – when, with the same ominous whir of muffled crepitation, another bullet whistled past us and this time actually ricocheted off the trunk above our heads. We both crouched down again. But when we once more raised our eyes, we saw that this second bullet had meekly rolled to a halt some twenty feet beyond the oak's girdling shadow – except that it was no bullet. Spherical, white and dimpled, it resembled nothing else on earth but what it all too manifestly was, a golf ball.

It dawned on both of us at the same time. Of course. A golf course. And everything now clicked into its logical place – the shapely pond, the suavity of the grass under our feet and finally, just at that instant, as if to resolve any last doubt that either of us might still have had, the faultlessly timed appearance of three male players trundling golf bags as vertical as vacuum cleaners across the horizon.

I scrambled to my feet.

'All right,' I said to Béa. 'If you want to go, let's go. But we have to go now. Even if Rieti wasn't shooting at us, it doesn't mean we've given him the slip.'

'Where shall we go?'

'If this is a golf course, there's bound to be a clubhouse.'

We decided to make a dash for it, an option rendered all the more urgent by the sudden sight of Rieti and Junior emerging on top of the slope which Béa and I had scaled a few minutes earlier. Convinced that we were being shot at, I had stupidly sacrificed the one advantage we'd had over them, that of time. Now we really would have to run for our lives. And, as we did precisely that, Béa's hand clutching mine, what, before, we had regarded only as lustrously sterile grassland was now seen to be chequered with sand traps like giant divots and glistening greens and holes with little flagpoles stuck inside them – I spotted number 13 as we rushed past it – and even tweedily dressed golfers, mostly in groups of twos and threes, one of them shouting some dated French obscenity at us when we crossed his field of vision just as, wiggling his rear end like a dog about to mount a bitch, he steadied himself to drive off. What *we* heard, though, was nothing to what our pursuers were forced to listen to when the same player, having seen the last of Béa and me, and impatient to pick up the thread of the game where it had been left off, was interrupted afresh by Rieti and Junior, and the whole rigmarole started over again.

The golf course seemed to be numerate, easily negotiable on foot, since, a little further forward from the thirteenth hole, we passed the twelfth and then the eleventh, the latter appropriated by a quartet of ladies in slacks, one of whom, on the point of taking a whack, was so rattled by our irruption on the scene she brought her club down hard on the very crown of the ball, which remained sitting on the tee as submissively as an egg in an eggcup. Then, however, quite unexpectedly, there was the fifteenth hole followed by the sixteenth. Change direction. I tugged Béa towards a nearby hillock on our right, above whose undulating spine I had already spotted the head and shoulders of a solitary elderly golfer in a tawny safari suit, one hand cupped over his brow, calmly watching the chase unfold beneath him. As we clambered up that hillock, there gradually swung into view, directly behind him, a single-storey, chalet-like pavilion on whose veranda a cluster of people, of both genders, stood with glasses of wine in their hands, looking up at the sky, scanning it for the prospect of rain. This, clearly, was the clubhouse I'd been seeking.

The covered veranda, tricked out with ornate, curlicued, vaguely Swiss motifs, ran the full length of the pavilion's slatted blue façade, and a dozen wicker chairs in the colonial style had been distributed from one end of it to the other. The only club members using these chairs were two middle-aged men, each dressed alike in a cashmere pullover, a paisley cravat, clean, crisp-creased jeans and suede loafers. Although neither of them was looking straight into the other's face, they were exchanging *basso profundo* whispers and weary mutual head-shakings. As Béa and I neared the veranda, gulping down our breathlessness while at the same time attempting to convey the impression of having just nonchalantly ambled in from the car park that must have adjoined the clubhouse, the man who was wearing the fancier of the two cravats glanced up in our direction. Without bothering to conceal the, to me, obvious fact that he was mentally stripping Béa, he turned on me a brief look of mild but not ill-disposed puzzlement, then turned back to listen to the companion who hadn't ceased to whisper in his ear.

The clubhouse had a small, low-ceilinged lobby, not unlike that of a gentleman's club, with striped linoleum flooring and, immediately on the right as one entered, a cloakroom-cum-reception desk. On the desk itself was a brass plaque which read *Réception: Mme Ginette Beauvois.* Madame Beauvois was seated behind the plaque but, as her head at that moment was bowed, it was to her mousy and tightly braided hairdo that I heard Béa, as she sailed past the desk, pulling me in her wake, call out a breezy 'Salut, Ginette!' As we continued on our way, I couldn't resist turning round to find out how Ginette had taken this, and I was just in time to see her, blinking with baffled disapproval over her bifocals, pick up what I presumed was the club's membership book and nervously flick through its pages.

It was when we entered the crowded bar that we both realised we had no notion what our next move should be.

'I'll get us a drink,' I quickly said to Béa, 'while you start thinking what to do now.'

Béa nodded and lit a cigarette. And I'd just started to head for the bar counter when I heard, above the genteel cacophony around us, a falsetto voice cry out to her in English, 'Béa? Why, it *is* Béa Cheret! Béa, it's me, it's

Shirley!' Cheerfully elbowing aside anyone who took too long to move out of her way, and dragging a ruddy-cheeked man behind her while he tried to shield with his left hand the gin-and-tonic he held in his right, ice cubes jangling inside the frosted glass, a woman approached us. Or, rather, an immense and all-embracing smile approached us, a smile so immense it appeared wider than the woman's face to which it was attached.

She enfolded Béa in a sticky hug. While the man and I stood by and surveyed one another with politely uncommunicative smiles, the two women embraced with that accursed hesitancy, familiar to anyone proffering a kiss to a Frenchman or Frenchwoman, as to who is kissing whom, and which cheek comes first, and is it to be once, twice, thrice or even – left cheek, right cheek, left cheek, right cheek – four times? Then Béa and the red-faced man kissed in their turn, just the once, a tangential peck.

Seen across a crowded room, I had guessed this woman, this 'Shirley', to be in her late thirties, or just turned forty, vivacious and bosomy. Even if the word 'brassy' had subliminally come to mind, I at once rejected it as much too unkind an epithet. Yet, as she thrust her way towards us, she seemed to age three or four years with every step taken; until, by the time she was standing right up against us – for she turned out to be one of those people whose habit it is to position themselves so close to whoever they chance to be talking to that the latter is constantly obliged to back off – by the time her face had become a mask of all too patently cosmetised comeliness and, where my own presence was concerned, undisguised curiosity, she could be seen to be frankly fifty if a day, and brassy after all, if still attractive. Embedded in her flesh like buttons in velveteen were two restless little eyes, at the corners of which, across the snowy terrain of her complexion, meandered a tell-tale trail of rambling avian footprints. She had kept her figure, though, her legs were nothing to be ashamed of, and she wore her smartly tailored salmon-pink suit with real panache.

As for the man I assumed was her husband, he had on a navy-blue, fur-collared jerkin half-zipped at the front over a striped tie that certainly looked as if it belonged to some old school or other, although I couldn't have said which. Beneath his bushy moustache his chin smelled vividly of aftershave. And he had pressed into heroic service, well beyond the call of duty, a few, far too few, horizontal strands of white hair to cover what would otherwise have been a broad bald patch on the top of his head.

'My dear,' said Shirley, addressing Béa but continuing to eye me, 'who'd have thought we'd meet here of all places! Didn't you tell me that golf bores you rigid?'

'It does,' said Béa quietly, adding, 'It's a long story, Shirley.'

'I'll bet it is,' said Shirley with relish. 'The best ones always are.'

She made great play of looking around her.

'Is Jean-Marc with you? I can't say I've noticed him.'

'No, he's in England. One of his trips.'

'I see . . .' – this said in such a fashion as to verge on the offensive, except that, under the circumstances, we had neither the time nor the nerve to be offended.

'Well?' Shirley continued imperturbably.

'Well what?'

'Aren't you going to introduce us?'

'Yes, of course, forgive me,' said Béa. 'Guy, I'd like you to meet two very dear friends of mine, Shirley and Oliver Knott. Shirley, Oliver – Guy Lantern.'

Our inopportune befrienders were a retired English couple who lived in Bournemouth and every other month would motor over to Normandy and Brittany to squander Oliver's generous pension on golf, gambling and good food. If Béa was acquainted with them, it was because Oliver – who, I was given to understand, had been something in the City, a stockbroker or investment adviser – had once purchased a painting from Jean-Marc, a landscape school of Corot, by a painter whose name I couldn't quite make out. It had subsequently turned out – not, I suspected, to entirely mutual gratification – that the Cherets had a villa in Saint-Malo, a town to which the Knotts had been coming 'since the year dot', as Shirley expressed it, and so a close friendship was born as haphazardly as many another.

When Béa introduced me, mention of my name caused Shirley to break into a high, pealing laugh that sounded affected even if it probably wasn't.

'Lantern. What a deliciously unusual name! Real, I suppose? Yes, of course it is, no one would ever make it up.

But what *can* it mean? That you come from a long line of lantern-makers, I daresay, though I must confess I never heard of such a profession. Still,' she went on, 'I should talk.'

Since I had no idea what the woman was referring to, I confined myself to a noncommittal grunt.

'Given my own name, I mean,' she replied with an encouraging nod.

'I beg your pardon.'

'Shirley Knott!'

For a second I thought she was rejecting my apology – then I got the point.

I chuckled dutifully. 'Of course. "Surely Not". How very awkward for you.'

She chuckled in her turn. 'But then, you see how handy it comes in as an icebreaker.' And, again taking note of my mystified expression, she explained, 'To break the ice? In conversations?' I smiled, and she added wistfully, 'Oddly enough, you'd think it would give rise to all sorts of awfully humorous misunderstandings. It never does, though, some-how.'

We all took time off for a moment in order to examine our footwear, until, brightening once more, Shirley asked, 'So how long have you known Béa?' – then, before I could answer, she said to Béa, with a flirtatious finger-wag, 'And how long did you expect to keep this young man to yourself?'

'Guy and I haven't known each other long. It's actually rather a marvellous story. Jean-Marc was driving –'

'Oh, Jean-Marc knows Guy, too?'

'Yes, of course he does,' replied Béa testily. 'What on earth is going through that head of yours, Shirley?'

'My head?' said Shirley, opening her eyes as wide as the two wee things could go. 'Why, nothing, Béa, nothing whatsoever. You know me.'

'I say,' said Oliver.

So very unlike him, up till then, was Oliver's having anything to say at all, Shirley, Béa and I all turned in his direction.

'I say,' he repeated gruffly, 'will you just look at that? Now what in God's name is *that* supposed to be? And what the hell's it doing here, is what I'd like to know.'

With the hand that was still wrapped around his glass of gin, he pointed at the doorway, where a loud verbal altercation had begun to brew up. Since the narrow interspace that had momentarily disclosed someone or something to him – the someone or something creating the problem – had already closed up again, it was difficult for the rest of us to know who or what had provoked it, as only those in its immediate neighbourhood, now fallen quiet with shuffling unease, would have been able to follow the slanging match of raised voices of which we, on the fringe, heard an unintelligible echo. Eventually, though, above an incessantly bobbing crest of heads, we all of us at the same time caught sight of a set of multicoloured spikes. Whether or not in his master's company, Junior had arrived.

Hastily proposing drinks all round, Béa started to shepherd

Shirley to the bar, arm linked in arm, leaving Oliver and myself to form, whether we wanted to or not, what felt like the male half of a double date. I noticed that poor Oliver was unable to prevent a shadow of dejection from flitting across his brick-red face, although he instantly replaced it, as soon as he saw that I'd seen it, with the generic, all-occasion beam of clubby male joviality.

' 'Shamed to have to admit it,' he said, as we prodded our way through to the far corner of the room, 'but, from what I could hear of his accent, that putrid young thug was British. How'd he fetch up here, do you suppose?'

'Search me,' I replied.

Having exhausted that line of conversation, 'Play golf, do you?' he then asked me.

Still trying to understand what was going on at the door, I replied any old how.

'Yes, I do.'

'Do you, though?' he said, seeming genuinely to cheer up, as if he had expected me to say no. 'Now there's a stroke of luck. Where do you play?'

'On a golf course.'

That, I knew at once, was not the correct answer.

'Is that so?' he said at last. 'And what's your handicap?'

'My handicap?' I affected to mull over the question for a moment. Then, my mind on other matters altogether, I mumbled, 'Two.'

'Two? Did I hear you say two?' He stared at me. 'Good Lord, that's . . . Well, well, you don't say. Two, indeed.'

And he twiddled one end of his moustache with such violence I feared he'd end by tying a knot in it.

(As it happens, I *had* played golf, although many years before, in my teens. My father was some sort of local champion, local meaning Haslemere and environs. And having once, for want of anything else to do, accompanied him on one of his tournament rounds and witnessed him down a hole-in-one – by chance, naturally – the ball peeking indecisively over the metallic rim of the cup for an eternity before taking the plunge, I had become so fired with enthusiasm for a sport in which miracles were not just possible but unavoidable, so I believed, as to decide, against all my usual, unathletic instincts, to take it up there and then. As in chess, though, so in golf there is, alas, no such thing as beginner's luck. I spent most of my time around the course grimly swinging a club back and forth in thickety under-growth in the hope that its burnished chestnut-hard head would at last connect with yet another of my many lost balls; and after only a couple of months, and no more than two complete eighteen-hole outings, the game and I parted company without regrets on either side. If I mention such a memory now, it's simply to show that I was well enough versed in the finer points of golf to realise that, on whatever type of course, two was an outlandishly small handicap for the no more than modestly gifted amateur I was supposed to be. But it was too late to withdraw the claim.)

We had meanwhile reached the bar and ordered our drinks, a kir for Shirley, whiskies for the rest of us. We stood there, hemmed in, sheltering our glasses from the piston-like acrobatics of neighbouring shoulders and elbows, and striving to make ourselves heard above the din. Although Shirley continued to monopolise the conversation, I heard only odd bits and pieces of what she was saying, my main concern being that Junior hadn't yet been ousted from the clubhouse, even if his spikes were no longer in sight. The whinnying hubbub at the far end of the room was still louder than it would have been had all been normal.

When, after a few minutes, I turned back to my own little party, the talk had turned to a film that the Knotts had recently watched on television, a Polish or Czech or Russian drama about the Holocaust.

'I'm sure it was part of a trilogy,' I heard Shirley say, 'but what was it called?' And she visibly racked her brains to retrieve the title, even poking a finger at her thickly powdered forehead in a gesture conventionally expressive of intense cerebral activity.

'It was *Road to . . . Road to . . .* Oliver, what *was* the name of the film?'

'What film was that, my love?' said Oliver, a hundred miles away.

'The one we saw at Deborah's. You know. About the librarian with specs who was sent to a concentration camp.'

'Ah, oh – *Road to Nowhere.*'

'Well, there you are, then,' said Shirley to Béa, 'I knew it was *Road to* somewhere. My dear, too tragic for words. On Christmas night, too,' she added enigmatically.

And she had begun to recount to Béa what seemed like the film's entire plot – the words 'swinish' and 'cattle-trucks' and 'the Kommandant or whatever you call him' floated in the air around us – when she came to a halt in abrupt mid-sentence. Bearing down on our little group with a princely hovercraft-smooth glissade, as if contriving not to touch the floor at all, was Rieti. A faint reddish swelling under his nose the only visible remnant of the Rolls's bumpy landing, he nodded at us benignly, smiling, smiling, all the while.

'My dear, good people,' he addressed us in his usual ornate manner, his eyes sliding off each of our faces in turn, 'profound apologies for trespassing on so festive a get-together, but I must exchange a word or two with Madame Cheret here. I would have preferred our chat to be in private and did indeed send my boy Junior in to communicate just such a message to her. Unfortunately, the tinpot officials of this establishment elected to send him packing before he was able to deliver it.'

'Junior?' said Shirley, who had got over her initial shock and seemed not to feel that she need now wait for an introduction. 'So that boy whose – whose hair we saw is your son?'

Rieti treated her to a look of amusement mingled with distaste.

'No, madame, he is not.' Then he said, 'I don't believe we've met. My name is Rieti.'

'Shirley Knott.'

'I must tell you, Mrs Knott,' he said – and, as Shirley had

foreseen, her name caused him not an instant of confusion –
'I must tell you, I am one of nature's bachelors. And yet,
too,' he added, 'a bachelor possessed of a strong paternal
instinct. Except that, having no sons of my own, I prefer to
have other people's sons, if you get my drift.'

If Rieti meant what I thought he meant, I seriously
doubted that Shirley did get his drift, for she merely gushed,
'Oh yes, yes of course, I know exactly what you mean.'

Rieti meanwhile turned towards the barman and said,
'Would you be so kind? A whisky, please.'

'On the rocks?' he asked, whisking a glass from somewhere beneath him.

'If you have any,' said Rieti with what might or might not
have been impudence: it certainly made the barman look up
sharply as he was about to prepare the drink.

'And what do you do, Mr Rienzi?' said Shirley.

'That's Rieti, madame, Rieti.'

'Rieti, of course. But what is it you do? For a living, I
mean? Or maybe you're so wealthy you don't have to make
a living?'

'Alas, no, that is not my case. Although I am the next best
thing – a friend to the wealthy. A Mr Nasr, to be specific.
Surely you've heard of him? You haven't? A Lebanese
gentleman – an industrialist, I suppose you would call him,
but he is even better known as a collector of artworks.'

'Aha,' said Shirley, with a meaningful look at Béa, 'I begin
to see the connection. Does he live in France, your Mr
Nasr?'

'No, no, not at all. In Kent. A charming old house.'

'I suppose he's very rich?'

'So rich, madame,' said Rieti dreamily, 'he pays other people to twiddle his thumbs for him.'

' "Pays other people to twiddle his thumbs" – why, how delightful!' exclaimed Shirley. 'And you say he lives in Kent? Where exactly in Kent would the house be? I have friends in Ashford – French,' she added solely for Béa's benefit, as if that fact would make them more interesting to her, 'the Larsonneurs, you remember them, I'm sure' – Béa shook her head – 'well, anyway, they live in Ashford. I mean, just outside Ashford. That's in Kent. Maybe' – to Rieti again – 'you've come across them?'

'No, madame,' he said, 'I haven't. I come across no one these days. My Mr Nasr's house is, you understand, nowhere. It's in the country. That's all that can be said about it. And that's its charm for Nasr – for myself, too, I might add. Thank you.' (This last to the barman, who had just handed him his whisky.)

'Don't you have company? Weekend house parties?'

'No again, madame. Proust is my only company. Which, I know you'll agree, is ample for anyone.'

Shirley nodded uncertainly, a minute red glow pinpricking each of her cheeks. Then she did what she no doubt always did when the conversation seemed to be escaping her: she changed the subject.

'You make regular trips to London, I suppose?'

'Very irregular trips. As irregular as humanly possible. And then, solely on business. You are looking at a hermit, a self-willed recluse.'

'But don't you miss the world? Don't you miss the restaurants, the theatres, the shops?'

I saw Rieti's face flicker with a not-so-secret glee, and I realised that, like some stand-up comic into whose long-baited trap a persistent heckler has finally, miraculously fallen, he had the perfect rejoinder tucked away in wait for just such a godsent *réplique*.

'For me, Mrs Knott,' he said, 'the world is like New York. It's a nice place to visit but I wouldn't want to live there.'

'How too killing!' said Shirley with a tinny squeal. 'My dear Béa, what a find he is! How *do* you do it?'

Whereupon, doubtless congratulating herself on having made a significant contribution to the success of our little gathering by inspiring, if not originating – which clearly wasn't her forte – such a conversation-stopping pearl, she seemed to decide that she could afford to fall silent for a while and let one of us others be given an opportunity to sparkle.

The silence was broken by Oliver.

'Play golf, do you?' he asked Rieti.

'Golf?' said Rieti, sipping his whisky carefully and eyeing Béa over the rim of his glass. 'Of course not.'

'We might organise a foursome,' Oliver went on, unabashed. 'You could rent the clubs, you know. Not expensive at all.'

'I didn't come here to play golf,' said Rieti, as if only a

moron would expect someone like him to be in the vicinity of golf links for the purpose of actually playing the game. 'As I say, I wish to have a word with Madame Cheret, if she is willing to spare me some of her time. Coincidentally, the chat we are due to have together is precisely about Mr Nasr. N'est-ce pas, madame?'

Béa stood calmly, clinking together the two or three melted ice cubes left in her near-empty tumbler, ice cubes which had wet their pants into the remaining *fond* of whisky, which was now of an unappealing uriny hue. Then, looking up at the ceiling-high window opposite us, a window from which a steeply raked sunbeam had enhaloed the hair on the backs of the heads of those guests who were standing nearest it, she said, 'Oh, we have all the time in the world to talk. I think a round of golf would be a terrific idea. Guy, you and I against Shirley and Oliver, eh? Come, Rieti, why don't you join us? A little fresh air is just what you need.'

'What I need, Madame Cheret . . .' he began. But he appeared to feel there was nothing for the moment to be done about the way the conversation was going and he began again. 'What I need is a cup of coffee. Refreshed, I'd be happy to join you on whatever jaunt you have in store for us. Provided, of course, that at the end of it all we shall have our tête-à-tête.'

'I promise you, Rieti, we'll have our tête-à-tête.'

'Well then,' he said to Shirley, 'and can a coffee be had in this club?'

'Why, yes, of course, as you see.' She pointed to a long

trestle table which had been laid out underneath the window and was presided over by a middle-aged woman with a name-tag pinned to her flower-print dress. On its starchy linen tablecloth sat a tall silver coffee-pot attended by a triple row of plain white china mugs.

'However, I ought to warn you, Monsieur Rieti,' she went on, 'the coffee here is just a tiny bit tasteless. It's all something of a factory, you see.'

'I don't drink coffee for its taste, dear lady. It's my petrol, my gasoline.'

'Ah, yes,' said Shirley with a beatific smile. 'So very, very true.'

And there being nothing more to add to that little manifesto of like-mindedness, we all repaired to the starchy white table.

When our coffees had been paid for, Oliver pressured by his wife into doing the honours, we trooped off to the clubhouse office where Béa and I were able to rent a pair of bags of rather seedy hand-me-down golf clubs.

Business at the first hole, and the one after, was much as might have been predicted. Oliver, the best player by far, would drive off as straight as if the ball were an arrow shot from a bowstring. Neither missing a short putt nor electrifying us all by sinking an indecently long one, he completed the two holes in a very decent nine. Shirley was more uneven but also more adventurous, compensating for a prolonged session in the rough of the first hole with a three on the second. Béa was a strange player. She would tranquilly place the ball on the tee, draw a club from the bag almost without looking to make sure it was the one she needed, gaze perfunctorily into the distance, raise the club with an arching sweep of her wrist and whack the ball as if it were a disagreeable something that she wished at once eliminated from her field of vision. It would soar upward and vanish into the void – then, suddenly, there it was again, rolling up the bank that gently sloped towards the green, if never quite making it to the top. As for me, I looked and felt every inch the novice I so nakedly was. And, as I could observe from the outset, from not much more than the way he studied my clumsily unorthodox grip, Oliver soon realised that my rashly claimed handicap of two had been so much fooling and pretending.

I might have fared better had I not been as preoccupied as I was by what, if immediately anything at all, should be done about our situation. Rieti, a discordant figure on the links in his silky black overcoat, started shadowing Béa and me everywhere we were obliged to go, deep into the rough if necessary. Or else he would head like a sheepdog for some spot equidistant from both of us, whenever, because of the vagaries of our play, she and I found ourselves wandering off in opposite directions. It was, moreover, on just one such scouting expedition of mine that, while attempting to liberate the ball from a clump of nettles amid which it sat like an obscene white mushroom, I looked up to discover, totally unobscured by the gangly-trunked tree behind which he deluded himself he was lurking, Junior following my every move.

Finally, at the third hole, things began to happen. When we had first walked out on to the course, Oliver had been generous to me with an old-timer's tips. 'Look out for that tricky curve at the twelfth . . .' he would advise me, or 'I think you may be amused by the seventeenth . . .' As I say, though, it had taken only a couple of amateurishly wild shots on my part for him to drop all pretence that he was playing with an equal, with someone who would know what he was talking about; from which point he had unresentfully, and more or less silently, resigned himself to competing with his own past and best performances rather than with Béa and me. Thus, on the third hole, without addressing a word to any of us, as if he were quite alone on the links, he drove off, this time just a trifle awry, the ball flying into the wind and promptly slanting to the left but probably, given his mundane, middling luck, coming to earth nowhere too inextricable. It was my turn next. Watched by Rieti, who was trying to light a cigar in the breeze, and by the two women, Béa keeping her own counsel, Shirley dabbing at her cheeks from a powder compact which she snapped shut with a click so loud and sharp it would have put me off my game had I had a game to be put off, I stood astride the ball as it cowered on its tee, swung my club as best I knew how and knew without even having to look, when the two of them made contact, that the crack which they produced together, the sort of crack one's inside hears when one breaks an arm or a leg, boded no good at all for its course down the fairway. And, sure enough, picked up by the wind between playful fingers, it proceeded to sail off to one side, hit the ground running, bounced once, hard and extremely fast, then pitched into a scrubby, overgrown copse located in that part of the course that was nearest the cliff.

Nearest the cliff ... and beyond the cliff, I suddenly realised, were the coastal road and the ocean. Oliver had begun to stroll towards the green. Shirley, whose turn it now was, paid no attention to either Béa or me, but stood astride the tee, peering now at the vista ahead of her, now down at the ball, now again at the vista, now at the ball. Rieti was still struggling with his recalcitrant cigar, which no sooner gained a hold on life than it would blow itself back out.

It was, I said to myself, now or never. Such an opportunity might not come my way again. My heart beating appallingly fast, I geared myself up to take the chance, one that chance itself, in the guise of a random throw of human dice, appeared to be holding out to me.

I looked towards Béa and whispered, as loudly as I dared, 'Béa! Béa!'

She turned. I nodded my head vigorously in the direction of the copse. 'Run, Béa, run!' I whispered, trusting that she would hear me and Rieti would not.

She heard me. Walking first at a normal speed, then very gradually accelerating, she and I began to head separately for the copse. Neither of us looked round, and there was no untoward muttering behind us to suggest that Rieti had noticed us tiptoeing from the stage. Then, about twenty or thirty seconds later, we heard Shirley, who had just driven off, cry out, 'Béa? Béa, where are you going?'

Knowing that, at the sound of her voice, Rieti too must have glanced up at last from his damp squib of a cigar, we let our walk finally and frankly transform itself into a run. Less audibly now, I heard Shirley say, in a tone of querulous put-upon reasonableness, 'Mr Rieti, I'm sure I don't like to be nosy, but there's obviously something between you and . . .' – and the rest was lost in the wind. As Béa and I raced towards the cliffline, its end-of-the-world dip beckoning three hundred yards ahead of us, I eventually turned to see what was happening. Rieti had also started to run, and from the far side of the course Junior had broken cover and was scurrying to catch up with him. Only Oliver, wandering by himself, already halfway down the fairway's pleasant green aisle, remained endearingly deaf and blind to everything going on about him.

It took us a few minutes to reach the same barbed-wire fencing through which we'd had to pull ourselves not more than an hour previously. Now, it being not the time for any shilly-shallying precautions, we tackled it head on. I shoved Béa in first, not even bothering to hold the wires apart. As I pulled my own self through, a last, impetuous tug left the torn flap of my jacket behind altogether, dangling from an especially devious knot that seemed to twitch at me with malice. From a little distance off, a wild goat scrutinised our progress with mild gum-chewing interest.

More than once, during our descent, I was convinced that Béa and I were about to fall head first. Some little local incline, slippery, swampy, still dank from past rainfall, would all of a sudden catch us unawares. Or our feet would become entangled in some tough clump of weeds. Or we would land on a bulge of slippery, moss-coated rock with the same unnerving thud as when one puts one's foot down on the phantom last-plus-one step of an unlit staircase. We helter-skeltered every which way, exploiting where possible whatever was already there under our feet, whether a narrow sandy path bordered on either side by thistles and dandelions in anarchic profusion or else, now fairly close to the bottom, an uninterruptible downhill stretch that encouraged us to take it at a frighteningly brisk run without giving us the means of braking that run once we had set out. It was on the very last stretch, in fact, when we were practically home, that we actually did fall, stumbling together on a black, hectagonal, lichen-enveloped boulder with roots sunk deep in the earth. And even if it was merely a schoolboy's fall, resulting in no more than bloodied kneecaps and bruised elbows, for one split, panicky second I closed my eyes tight and was transported to another disaster, to another fall, and I saw again the arch of trees, the snowman in the field, and Ursula's shattered face.

Picking ourselves up, we turned at exactly the same moment to glance behind us. Near the summit of the hill Rieti and Junior were making their way along a transversely descending slope, Rieti clutching Junior by one of the chains of his punkish gear and Junior assisting him down step by step, placing himself, as we watched, on a level just under Rieti's own the better to receive him in his embrace, in a rush, like a parent catching his tiny offspring.

Then, suddenly, their exertions ceased. For some reason Rieti did not drop, as expected, into Junior's waiting arms but remained standing on what I imagined was a little mud-calloused plateau. He was watching us looking up at him. Although I couldn't see his face distinctly, nor he either of ours, our eyes nevertheless contrived to meet across the full declivity of the cliffside. For a paralysing instant – and even if the Rolls was just yards away from us now – neither Béa nor I moved a muscle. Then Rieti raised his right arm at a ninety-degree angle to his body and I noticed with interest that he was holding, in the palm of his hand, some bulky black object like a cordless phone. Just as I gazed up at it, trying to figure out what it could be, it exploded with a flash and a bolt of lightning struck my left shoulder.

I lost consciousness – but it couldn't have been for more than a few seconds, for, when I came to, I found myself still groggily on my feet, and Rieti standing just where he had been before I had blacked out. My shoulder, though, felt nauseatingly gummy, and a snaky tributary of what could only have been my own blood was already starting to fill the cup of my armpit. An ashen-cheeked Béa was at my side, gripping my elbows, and I heard her say something like 'Oh God, oh God, oh God, you've been hit!'

Myself I heard answer, 'It's nothing, it's nothing, it's only a flesh wound.' But the words came out thick and coagulated, for my upper lip was as stiff as if it had been anaesthetised. I couldn't resist poking a finger into the tear that the bullet had slashed open in my jacket. The pain was so harrowing it made my eyes water, but even I, although inexperienced in these matters, could tell at once that the viscously fleshy mess I felt underneath my shirt was no more than a superficial laceration.

'Guy – are you able to walk?' said Béa anxiously.

'Yes . . . yes of course I am,' I said. 'The pain is murder, but I think it really is only a flesh wound.'

'Then take my arm. Quick – we've got to get out of here.'

With a tremendous effort, limping madly in a feeble attempt to dodge whatever bullets Rieti might still have had left up the sleeve of his revolver (but apparently there were none), I managed to scuttle to the car. And, after a few wheezy coughs and splutters, when the listing Rolls struggled desperately to clear its throat, we were away.

Now we were on the very last stretch, no more than twenty minutes, I reckoned, from Mont Saint-Michel. Since there was little chance of finding a doctor on the way, and since, too, Béa didn't care to have me answer awkward questions about my injury before she had recovered the painting, we decided to stick to our original plan. She meanwhile took the only cigarette left from the packet in the glove compartment, ironed out its wrinkles with a scabrous gesture of her thumb and forefinger and, after first taking a long, slow puff on it herself, handed it to me. I had the feeling that she was speeding, certainly driving faster than before. But the speedometer told me different.

Although the bleeding seemed to have dried up, my shoulder ached badly, and my head worse. The headache, worst of all, was no longer a generalised soreness but had nastily homed in to the little bas-relief protuberance of my right eyebrow, which felt tender and migrainous.

It was just when I started to suspect I might have a fever that I cast a glance at the stretch of coastline lying ahead of us. A few hundred yards away, a pedestrian walkway which had been running alongside us for most of our journey, separating the coastal road itself from a ridge of jagged black rocks, curved off on to an even narrower footpath which, yet another few hundred yards or so further along, abruptly extended itself out over the corrugated surface of the ocean like a pier. At the end of this footpath there could be seen a strange, stunted column or tower in the exact shape of a tumescent penis. It had two slit-like windows on the side that was visible to us, one of them close to its conical coolie's-hat roof and the other virtually on the ground. The latter window was so low, indeed, I couldn't be sure it was a window at all, for the tower's inhabitants, whoever they might have been, would have had to crawl on all fours if they had hoped to look out of it. And just as had happened to me once or twice already, but I had neither the time nor the clarity of mind to recall where or when, I had the sensation that I'd somehow seen it all before, that I was obscurely acquainted with its four-square stonework, its brooding, phallic thereness. It wasn't new to me, nor was it familiar. It was, rather, as if it were its very unfamiliarity with which I had come to feel familiar.

Then it was gone. I hesitated a long while before speaking to Béa about the sensation, for I didn't want to make too much of what might have been nothing more than a febrile figment of all my various and still churningly active aches and pains. In fact, I waited until it had completely disappeared from view, then started to say, 'Béa, I –'

But by then it was too late. We had already quit the coastline and turned inland. The ocean was nowhere now to be seen. We were driving through one of those lifeless villages of northern France as hard to tell one from the other as the innumerable small towns that dot the American hinterland. As we motored along its torpid main thorough-fare, I spotted a deserted café that might either have been open or closed for all anyone seemed to care, a general store whose airless and antiquated window display offered a jumble of dated little girls' dresses, reels of coloured wool, china ornaments and cheap plastic toys that no child could ever have coveted, and a jerry-built supermarket whose already barbarous Franglais name had been aggravated by a gratuitous apostrophe *s* that grated on my peripheral vision like a speck of grit in the corner of the eye. Apart from three parked cars, the road through and out of the village was devoid of traffic. And it was when we ourselves had driven a mile or so out of it that Béa suddenly said to me, 'Look, Guy, look.'

There, on the horizon, was Mont Saint-Michel — rising from the sea, my guidebook had lyrically put it, 'like the answer to a prayer', and to France, as Victor Hugo once wrote, 'what the great pyramid is to Egypt'. I had seen a hundred snapshots of Mont Saint-Michel. I knew its contours as well as I knew those of the Baptist church at the end of my own street at home. Yet it's one of those landmarks that, irredeemably clichéd as they have become, never quite forfeit the capacity, as soon as one is actually there, in front of them, sharing their space, as they say, to take one by surprise. It's the very fact of *being there* that is the source of one's wonderment. Not that *they* are there, but that *one* is there.

Beyond Mont Saint-Michel there was nothing — nothing but a blank, unfilled-in backdrop, a shimmering, horizonless emptiness which betrayed the offstage presence of an ocean unheard and unseen. In consequence, for as long as we were approaching it, the Mont appeared to rise not from the sea, as my guidebook had it, but from the earth, from the very soil of France, and our view of it as we drove through a countryside so trim and green and geometrical it resembled more the ordnance map of a region than the region itself, reminded me of a photograph I'd been given as a child, of an oil tanker gliding along the Suez Canal, a photograph taken at so ingenious an angle as to convey the illusion of a ship ploughing through dusty yellow cornfields. The road in front of us was relatively straight, the landscape on either side flat and low-lying, and as we drew closer to our destination, eventually arriving at the causeway that would carry us across, and the whole monstrous construction began to tower over us, from the soaring ball-point tips of its spires to the batwinged archangel surmounting the tallest spire of all, it befuddled our every instinctive intuition of distance and space.

Only when we were actually crossing the causeway did I discover a less monolithic Mont Saint-Michel. Seen that close to, it turned into a mere monument, a tourist trap like any other on the planet, the only difference being that the tourists here, who might well have been the same I'd already encountered a couple of days before in Saint-Malo, seemed to be trapped in a never-ending circuit of regression. I saw them, through the Rolls's windscreen, climb up the island's winding streets and stairways, up, up, up, towards the abbey – and yet, always, mysteriously, there they were back again, on exactly the same level from which they had set out, come full circle, or full spiral, like the droll mannikins in one of Escher's fantasies of logic-defying circularity.

I turned to Béa.

'You say Sacha has a studio here. Surely nobody *lives* on Mont Saint-Michel?'

'Oh yes they do. Not many, about a hundred and fifty inhabitants, I think. They're called Miquelots, or Montois, something like that. Sacha inherited the studio from his father, who lived in it like a recluse all his life.'

'Odd spot for a recluse to choose to live, wasn't it? One of the most famous monuments in the world?'

'You don't know Mont Saint-Michel. I can't explain to

you, Guy, how it can be so, but it's a place that's somehow both open and very, very secret. I promise you.'

A minute later we had crossed the causeway and arrived in a car park in which scores of cars were disposed in symmetrical rows. It being that ambiguous and quasi-autumnal moment of late afternoon when the sole red orb to be seen in an ill-defined sky could either have been a late sun setting or a premature moon in ascendancy, most of the Mont's visitors were now pouring out into the car park through a tall granite gate that opened up in its outer wall and was its only entrance and exit. It was there that Béa and I made our way on foot.

We entered a small cobblestoned courtyard; then passed through a second gate, into a second courtyard; then a third gate, the last, which brought us out on to the Mont's steep and sinuous main street. Béa quickly started climbing this street, whose houses were so lopsided with age and disrepair they seemed to be leaning out of their own windows. There were souvenir shops and pizzerias and ever more souvenir shops; but I also saw on our left, as we ascended, La Mère Poularde, which made me think again of Rieti and Junior. As we rose, the abbey, after momentarily disappearing from sight, would suddenly reappear, drawing itself up to its full height, the slate-grey tiles of its topmost spire bleached by the fading sunlight.

Instead of mounting the now lamplit stairway to the basilica, instead of accompanying those straggling last-call visitors on the way up and crossing the paths of the far more numerous others on the way back down – none the wiser, I would have said, from their pilgrimage – Béa turned off past an allotment of threadbare grass and into a fetid alleyway so constricted, so claustrophobic, our shoulders literally scraped against its walls. From its other end we emerged, quite alone, into a little medieval square dominated by an elegantly dilapidated building over whose doorway an eighteenth-century street lamp swayed with a regular and softly repetitious creak. Here she came to a halt.

'Sacha's studio is on the top floor of this building,' she said to me in a calm voice. 'Now, Guy, I know you're not going to approve, but I have to speak to him alone.'

'You will not,' I replied. 'We've come this far together, and now you tell me you're going to face the worst part of it all, the climax, by yourself. It's out of the question. We're going in together or not at all.'

'Be reasonable. Alone, I know I can handle him. You forget – it's you who are the problem. If you insist on coming in with me, who knows what will happen – to us and to the painting.'

'Then tell me why I'm here at all.'

'That was your decision, Guy, not mine. I *will* need you – but not now, not at once. I've got to get into his studio and I can only do that if you stay down here.'

She had a point. I muttered a few formulary protestations, but I already knew her well enough to know that if she'd made up her mind there could be no contradicting her.

When she pressed a button on the wall, the building's

front door flung itself open as if it had been unlocked in his sleep by some napping concierge. The dark ground-floor entryway, a glimpse of which I caught as she slipped inside, emitted an indefinable but probably feline and, whatever it was, disreputable aroma. Béa walked off along the corridor, turned to the right and disappeared. I listened intently as she mounted a short flight of wooden stairs. The squeaky crescendo of her footsteps receded to the first-storey landing, at which point the dull muffle of flagstone flooring took over for exactly four steps. Then she was on the rise again, although increasingly faintly, and when she reached the second storey she moved out of earshot altogether. There was total silence. For the next minute or thereabouts, I attempted to resign myself to waiting in the street, holding the door open with my foot; finally, incapable of bearing the suspense a second longer, I stepped right inside, letting it slam shut behind me. The corridor was humid with cat's urine and its walls flaunted all the shabby discolouration of neglect. Peering up from the depths of the ground floor, I saw, at the very top of the stairwell, approaching the third and final landing, a nervously flitting shadow. I was able to make out one last footfall, followed by a shuffling noise, as of someone taking a lungful of air before committing an irrevocable act, followed by silence again. Then the whisper of a knock.

No answer. The knocking grew louder. A door handle was tried. I listened as it rattled first one way – then, quite pointlessly, as Béa must have known, the other. But there was no opening of any door.

I heard Béa's voice: 'Sacha? Sacha?'

Silence.

'Sacha!'

Silence again, save for the low rumble of persistent knocking.

'Sacha, c'est moi. C'est Béatrice. Laisse-moi rentrer, s'il te plaît. *S'il* te plaît.'

I had to strain more and more to hear what was being said.

'S'il te plaît, chéri. Je sais bien que tu es là. Alors, ouvre-moi. Il faut qu'on se parle.'

Suddenly, from behind the locked studio door, and so violently I felt the force of his rage from the foot of the stairs, I heard Sacha cry, 'Aaaaah, fous-moi le camp! Tu m'emmerdes! Tu m'emmerdes, je te dis!'

I could almost see Béa's cheek right up against the door.

'Veux-tu ouvrir la porte? Rien n'a changé, rien. C'est toujours nous deux, toi et moi, ensemble, comme je t'ai promis – pour toujours. Tout ce que je t'ai toujours promis. S'il te plaît.'

A series of locks began to be warily unbolted. I imagined a pencil-slim crack opening in the door, wide enough for Sacha to verify that Béa was alone on the landing. I imagined their eyes meeting. And, when I then heard a loud scuffling, I imagined Béa, taking no chances, pushing the door forward to force her way in and Sacha struggling to close it again, both of them tumbling sometimes backward into the studio and sometimes back out on to the landing.

The time had come for me to intervene. Without waiting for any call of assistance from Béa, I ran upstairs, two at a time, the irregular creaks of rotten wood under my feet giving me away more surely than if I had shouted up in advance that, ready or not, I was on my way. On the dingy third-storey landing Béa and Sacha were screaming at each other. He was wearing a long, stringy pullover smeared with paint and a pair of scruffy white flannels whose turn-ups had been doubly, even triply, rolled up over bare feet as hirsute as those of a chimpanzee. When he saw me, over Béa's shoulder, he cried out, 'Vous! Bien sûr. J'aurais dû deviné. Eh bien, non! Je dis non, non et non! Vous ne l'aurez jamais, vous deux – jamais! Je préfère le brûler!'

Contorted with rage, he threw Béa against a banister so rickety I thought she was about to pitch head first into the stairwell. Then he lunged at me, grinding his teeth, lashing out in all directions, pounding my head with a scattershot shower of incontinently ineffectual blows. Caught off guard, I first went on the defensive. Attempting to shield my wounded shoulder from those two fists of his which kept looming up at me in hallucinatory, hairy-knuckled close-ups whenever I opened my eyes, I found myself blinded by my own hands. Gradually, though, I managed to control my reflexes. I even began to gain the upper hand, able no longer just to ward off his punches but to return them. I made tentative jabs at his abdomen, then at his hollow chest, then more confidently at his chin. Dragging his feet, forced, step by grudging step, to back into the studio, he hit his heel against a thin strip of metal demarcating the line of the threshold and hovered for a few seconds at a crazy acute angle before righting himself. Then, with a lunatic's speed and agility, he swivelled about, made a dash for a large mahogany chest of drawers which had been shoved against one of the studio's walls next to a stacked-up pile of yellowing magazines, gave its top drawer so superhuman a tug it came right off in his hands and drew a small black pistol out of it. As he aimed it at me, I leapt forward and, without thinking what I was doing, butted him hard on the neck. I made a direct hit on his prominent, pebbly Adam's apple, whose bump, like the pip of a berry, I heard go pop against my skull. With an ugly gurgling groan Sacha stared at me, all malevolence drained from his face. Then his legs went limp and he began to collapse. Instinctively, I leaned over to grab him, but my shoulder was too stiff to react with the necessary flexibility and I could only look on helplessly as, one of his bare toes catching on some unseen groove in the carpetless floor, he twisted his body sideways and, falling, cracked his head hard against the bevelled edge of the chest of drawers. It was all over. He crumpled to the ground and lay there unconscious, his legs splayed out in front of him like those of a dummy propped up in a ventriloquist's dressing room; his head, also like a dummy's, flopping forward on to his filthy pullover; the pistol flying across the floor and careening into the pile of magazines.

I closed the door behind me and took stock of the room. Sacha's studio was neither small nor large, it was squarish to the point of boxiness and had almost no furniture. The only source of light was a naked overhead bulb which, the front door having been left open to the hallway for several minutes, was swinging to and fro in its socket, transferring its cold spotlight from Béa to myself and back again, via an unexceptional patch of wall to which, for an instant, it would direct abrupt and unmerited attention. There was also a wall lamp, a plain, plastic hemisphere, above the chest of drawers. Apart from that chest, on which sat a flower-like, four-stemmed candelabrum, all four petals of one of whose pink glass crocuses had been plucked, there was a cane-bottomed chair of the primitive type painted by Van Gogh (underneath it two twin pairs of black town shoes were tidily arrayed) and an artist's easel erected on a tripod base. The paint-smudged walls had started to peel, and the spaces between the floorboards, on which Sacha's body lay sprawled, were as caked with dirt as his bare toenails.

As I took it all in, my scalp started to tingle. My forehead was drenched in sweat and the palms of my hands looked as if they'd been whitewashed.

'Guy, do you know you've gone deathly pale?' said Béa at last, staring into my face. 'Is it your shoulder?'

'No.'

'Sacha?'

'No . . . I don't know . . .'

'You mustn't torment yourself, it was self-defence. I saw how it happened. You didn't intend to hurt him.'

'No, no, no. It – it isn't that at all.'

'Then what is it? What's the matter with you?'

'I tell you I don't know. I mean, it's impossible. Yet . . .'

'Yet what?'

'Well, it's just . . . It's just that I feel I've been here before. Here, inside this room.'

There was a pause. Béa's eyes locked into mine. She seemed not to know what to say next.

Finally, putting out the naked overhead light and switching on the wall lamp, she murmured quietly, 'Yes. You're right.'

'What do you mean?'

'It *is* impossible.'

I remained as if petrified, statufied. Then Béa spoke again.

'We haven't any time to waste. We've got to find the painting and get out of here before he' – she looked down at poor Sacha – 'before he comes to.'

'So you know where it is?'

'Rolled up in the bottom drawer of that chest of drawers. That's where he always kept it. Open it, will you.'

I tried the drawer.

'It's locked,' I said dully.

She shook her head in mock-disbelief.

'Locking a drawer in an apartment in which he lives alone!' She began to tap the various pockets of her suit, like someone frisking herself. 'Thank God I decided it would be wiser for me to have a key made for myself.'

Béa was standing in front of the chest of drawers, to the side of the candelabrum. Not one of its crocus-shaped bulbs was lit; but now, above it, the wall lamp *was* lit, shedding a more powerful light than might have been expected from so puny a fitting and casting its glow from beneath over the lower half of Béa's face. I was standing beside her, waiting for her to give me the key to the chest of drawers. Between us, on the wall behind the lamp, there was the room's only window, its pane unwashed for many a month. There was nothing to see out of it, though, but a dark, cloudy, red-tinged sky, the sea plashing invisibly beyond the confines of the frame.

Béa removed from her jacket pocket a small pouch or purse made out of some kind of beigey-brown fur.

'Here it is. Try the bottom drawer, will you. I'm positive you'll find the canvas there.'

She held out the pouch or purse in her right hand.

From its shape and its size and the asymmetric indentations on its surface, it was obvious, even had Béa not told me, that it contained a key.

I froze.

Suddenly I knew everything.

' "La Clé de Vair" is a fake.'

I gave Béa no chance to answer me. I took the key out of the pouch – it was an ordinary brass key – walked over to the

[*160*]

chest of drawers, unlocked the bottom drawer, pulled it open and found the rolled-up canvas just as Béa had said I would. I lifted it out – I cannot say what Béa was doing all the while I did this for I was too terrified to look in her direction – went to the easel and stretched the painting over it. I gazed at it. It was the mirror image, only reflected back three hundred years into the past, of exactly how she and I had been positioned a moment before. I turned to face Béa and, in a neutrality of tone that only just succeeded in holding the lid down on my excitement, I told her what I now knew to be true.

' "La Clé de Vair" is a fake. It wasn't painted by Georges de La Tour. It wasn't painted in the seventeenth century. It was painted here – and not all that long ago. The room in the painting is this room. The light in the painting . . .' – I pointed to the delicately painted shaft of light on the canvas, so typical of La Tour's work – '. . . is the light from this lamp . . .' – and I pointed to the wall fitting. 'The island framed by the window . . .' – I pointed to the one aspect of the décor which, in the black-and-white reproduction I'd examined back at the villa, I had been unable to make out but which I could now see from the canvas itself was a window – '. . . is the island I saw when we were driving along the coastal road. The tower . . .' – I pointed again – '. . . is the tower I noticed just before we turned off the coastal road. And the woman in the picture – you are that woman, aren't you? It was you who posed for the artist, wasn't it?'

Béa didn't answer.

'And here,' I said, jangling the unprepossessing little object before her, 'here is the key. La Clé de La Tour.'

I detected no clear sign that Béa was assimilating anything I had said. By then, however, it had ceased to matter all that much, as I was as certain of the scenario I had just presented to her as I have ever been of anything in this world. But I was determined that it wasn't going to be I who would speak first and, as we stood facing each other, my eyes strayed towards a closed door at the far end of the room. Neither of us having yet said a word, I went to open it. It was the door to Sacha's studio proper. Illuminated by a large oriel window which laid bare the ocean and the sky, the vista split in two by the moonlight-mottled horizon, this second room had even less furniture than the other. In the centre stood another empty easel, but my attention was attracted beyond it to a stack of canvases piled up against a wall. Even from a distance, the visible, topmost one was calculated to catch the eye. Partially concealed by the tripod's three spindly limbs, its two hind legs akimbo like those of Henry VIII, it was a painting of a gigantic blue cauliflower sprouting from a nocturnal vegetable garden under a doomful yellow moon. It was a startling enough image in its way, yet also a poor, tame cliché, the cauliflower's curls and folds executed with scary meticulousness in a viscid shade of aquamarine.

I knelt over the stack and, despite the clunkiness of their thick wooden supports, began to riffle through the canvases like a bank teller counting off a wad of used hundred-pound notes. There were six of them, and all had been painted by the same person, someone not without real technical flair but, as it struck me at once, hopelessly in thrall to Dali for the paintings' ugly, oleaginous textures and to Magritte for their subject-matter – rather, for the collection of tawdry conceits, the commonplaces of hand-me-down surrealism, with which the artist had vainly sought to camouflage the absence of true and personal subject-matter. The five that were concealed by the cauliflower consisted of a head-and-shoulders portrait of a top-hatted middle-aged man whose facial features were obscured by a fried egg; a revolver that fired doves; a long-faced, two-humped animal with a head at each end of its torso and the cute neologism 'palindromedary' stencilled beneath it; a painting of the Crucifixion whose own canvas had been nailed on to a cross, phony painted blood seeping from its three nail-wounds; and an otherworldly skyscape of a frothy bank of clouds that turned out to be, as one studied them, the four Presidents' heads from Mount Rushmore.

I set the canvases back in place and remained as I was for a moment or two. Then my eyes strayed again, more consciously, as I was now on the lookout for clues, and I noticed that a score of charcoal drawings had been pinned up higgledy-piggledy in another corner of the room. These I went to inspect. Some of them were portraits à la Modigliani; some were cunning cribs of Matisse, Soutine and Bonnard. There was, too, what looked like a half-hearted and prematurely abandoned stab at a prettified Ingresque compo-sition of the Three Graces – three fashion-plate nudes, arms duly interlinked, with embryonically sketchy yet unmistakably identical faces and bodies. As for the other drawings, which comprised more than half of the total, they were all preliminary studies, complete with period costume trappings, of the female figure from 'La Clé de Vair'. Nor could there be the slightest doubt that each of the women depicted – the Modiglianis, the Matisse, the Soutine and the Bonnard, all three of Ingres's naked triplets and, by now screamingly obvious, the La Tour – was Béa.

I returned to the first room. Béa hadn't moved. She seemed to be waiting for me to ask again the same question that I'd already put to her. But it was for her to speak, and she eventually did.

'Yes, you're right,' she said without a tremor. 'It is a fake.'

'So why don't you tell me about it?'

She looked at me as if making sure I really wanted to know the truth, and something, or its shadow, darted swiftly over her face, something coarse and hard and mercenary I'd never seen in it before.

'It was painted – this, I know, you've figured out for yourself – by Sacha. Sacha's a painter – I mean, he was a painter, before he became Jean-Marc's partner. He's never had the least success, not once, not ever. I presume you've been examining his work, so I don't have to tell you why. He's always possessed an extraordinary facility, but what he does, and it's all he can do, is hopelessly out of fashion – worse still, his paintings always make you think of somebody else's, Dali's or Max Ernst's or Magritte's.' She cast her eyes around the dirty and deeply depressing monk's cell of a room in which we were standing. 'The gods played a horrible practical joke on Sacha. They gave him the hands of a genius, but it's as if those hands were grafted on – like in a horror movie. He's never had a spark of individuality or originality. He knows how to paint, but he hasn't the faintest notion what to paint or, more to the point, why to paint. And what makes it a thousand times worse is that he knows better than anybody just how trivial and superfluous his talent is. He's like a man born blind who suddenly discovers he can actually imagine, he can *visualise*, what it is to see.

'Anyway, he started drawing me in different styles, the modern Ecole de Paris, mostly – I have to say,' she laughed drily, 'they were the easiest. It started as a little game just between the two of us. Or perhaps for him it was also a way of expressing his desire for me. It was his way of courting me, I suppose, and frankly I was flattered. Then, oh, about two years ago, when I don't think he was even aware of what he'd achieved, he made a gorgeous drawing of me in the style of Georges de La Tour. I was absolutely stunned by it. I encouraged him, and he worked at it and worked at it until nobody, I swear, could have told it from the real thing – except, if course, there wasn't any real thing. Not a single drawing exists by La Tour.

'I knew I couldn't bear much more of my life with Jean-Marc, but there was no question of leaving him without taking measures in advance to secure my future. So, at first for a giggle, when neither of us knew whether the other was really serious, Sacha and I devised the plan. He would paint a Georges de La Tour, which we'd then sell to one of Jean-Marc's clients.'

'Was Jean-Marc in on your plan?'

'Of course not. But even though he had nothing to do with it, for us there was no better guarantee of the painting's authenticity than his own standing in the art world.'

'Why Nasr?'

'He's an ignorant man, a know-nothing, who happens to have more money than he will ever be able to spend. Over the years, I must tell you, Jean-Marc has palmed off on Nasr all sorts of duds at inflated prices – either second-rate works by second-rate artists or third-rate works by first-rate artists. Heaven only knows how many times he swindled him. We were simply going to take the process a logical stage further.'

'But there's something I don't get,' I said. 'It was *this* painting – or a print of it – that I saw in the book in your villa. It was *this* room. It was *your* face.'

'The only reason Sacha wrote the book was to lend credence to the existence of the painting.'

'What!'

'Let me tell you, Guy, writing the book was nothing compared to painting the picture. Sacha is a real expert on the seventeenth-century French school.' She laughed again. 'His reputation was the only authentic thing about the whole business.'

'To write a book . . .'

'Why are you surprised that we'd go to such lengths?

Think what was at stake. Painting "La Clé de Vair" took Sacha the best part of two years. We had to find paints and canvas materials that were consistent with La Tour's period. I had to spend hours, days, in libraries poring over fashion histories. A single error in one of the costumes and we'd have been done for. Believe me, the book was the least of it.'

'Was it actually published?'

'It was privately printed in Belgium. That was the fun part. We invented the publisher's name, wrote the blurb, cooked up an ISBN number. I've never forgotten it. 0–436 204 290.'

'And Jean-Marc?'

'Jean-Marc?'

'He knew of the book's existence?'

'He thought it had been published in England. In Cambridge. He was madly jealous when I took a copy of it to Nasr, the one time I accompanied Jean-Marc to Kent. You see, Nasr had to have the book in his library before we dared to broach the possibility of his buying the picture. It all went like clockwork – until that fucking tree was struck by lightning.'

'So that's why you couldn't let Rieti enter this room?'

'If Rieti had seen what you've just seen, if he'd come face to face with Sacha himself . . .'

'Oh God . . .'

I was trying desperately to know what I felt at that instant. I knew I wanted still to be hers, still to be at her side, on her side, and I can't deny, either, that what she had just told me had filled me with a certain elation, the elation known to every bearer of thrillingly bad news. But it *was* bad news, it surely was bad news, and it could only end in crisis, disaster and maybe death. Béa had to be saved from herself, from Sacha, from the incalculable consequences of their *folie à deux* – but before I could express anything of what I felt, she had already approached me and clasped her hands around my neck.

'Don't forget what you said, Guy,' she whispered, as if afraid that Sacha might overhear her. (Sacha? Sacha? Why don't you open your eyes?) 'You promised you'd never judge me. Well, I mean to hold you to that promise. I won't be judged. I did what I had to do, which is what life is all about.'

'Whose theory of life is that?'

'Nothing has changed,' she said – and I recalled how she had used the same phrase, *rien n'a changé*, when she inveigled Sacha into unlocking his door to her. 'What does it matter that "La Clé de Vair" is a fake? That's a detail. It's certainly not a reason for not selling it to Nasr. He won't know the difference. I tell you, men like him don't know differences.'

It was then, finally, on hearing these words, that I understood how I could turn her own argument against her, how I could make her see that, even now, it wasn't too late for her to draw back from the disastrous adventure on which she had embarked.

Yes, I cried, nothing *had* changed, and that was what would save her. No real crime, after all, had yet been committed. 'La Clé de Vair' could be destroyed and the money already deposited in Béa's account returned to Nasr. It would be an unpalatable business, and it would probably entail the risk of physical violence to both of them. They could only hope – but it was a reasonable hope – that, preferring not to compromise his status as an alien in Britain, Nasr would be willing to write off the whole sorry affair to experience. Then Béa and I could be together, without the ever-present fear of retribution.

'What would prevent us from being happy?'

Béa slowly withdrew her hands from my neck and looked down at Sacha's long, lean body. After a pause, she knelt over him and placed the side of her head against his chest. She listened for a few seconds, eyes rapt but unfocused, then raised his right arm, which his fall had caused him to fling out wide in a posture of childlike innocence and plenitude. She held it aloft as if weighing it and let it drop again with a sickening thud. I swallowed hard. Inside me, I could feel something obscene bubbling up from my abdomen, rising into my throat and threatening to choke me. She raised her eyes and, without a trace of emotion in her voice, said, as I already knew she was going to, 'Sacha's dead.'

I thought I was about to faint. I closed my own eyes and a display of hellish fireworks silently exploded in the caverns of my eyelids. I opened them again. Béa was still kneeling by Sacha's body.

'You're lying,' I said.

'He's dead. His heart has stopped beating and his pulse –

you can feel it for yourself. He must have cracked his skull when he fell.'

She started to cradle his head, supporting it at the nape of his neck, but immediately dropped it. The palm of her hand was slicked with half-dried, toffee-apple-like blood. She held it out towards me.

'Now a real crime *has* been committed. We can't go back, either of us.'

I had to do something, say something, quick.

'You're mad. You saw what happened. It was self-defence – an accident.'

'Like the accident that killed your wife?'

I recoiled like someone who had been shot in the heart. The obscene fluid which I could feel rising up through my insides had now invaded my throat. I struggled to remain lucid. I found myself waiting, waiting for Béa to say something that would at once erase what I nevertheless knew was an indelible stain. I found myself wondering if there existed in the English language's infinitely untapped potential a configuration of nouns, verbs and adjectives that in just the right combination could somehow repair the fatal damage.

If such a configuration does exist, it eluded her.

'Darling Guy,' she said in a pragmatically unflustered voice, as if my horror were no more than dawning comprehension on my part of the parlous plight I'd got myself into, 'like it or not, that's the sort of thing somebody is bound to say. The police are going be nosing about our affairs sooner or later, and they'll be digging up what they can about both of us –

and what happened to you and Ursula is sure to come out. I don't know exactly what they're going to think, what connections they're going to try and draw, but I can imagine. Even if they accept your version of events, and it would have to include your meeting with Jean-Marc, the swapping of cars, the flash of lightning – the flash of lightning, Guy! just think, would you believe that story if you were in their shoes? – it will be the end of you. We've *got* to go on. Besides,' she added thoughtfully, 'Sacha's death may be a blessing in disguise. He was the only person who could have given us away.'

'How can you speak of him like that? The man was your lover.'

'Sacha meant nothing to me. I told you, he was convenient.'

'And his dying in that way was just one of life's little inconveniences?'

'For God's sake, Guy, don't weaken now, now that we're nearly home – now that there are just the three of us.'

'The three of us?'

Her smile sent a shiver through me.

'Just you, me and the money. We can go wherever we like, do whatever we like – and do it as often as we like.' Then, abruptly, her voice changed again. 'But, listen, if we don't move now, it will all have been for nothing.'

'You *are* mad,' I said.

'No, I'm not mad. I'm just trying to keep my head. As long as no one suspects we were ever here, we'll be all right.

Sacha was a loner, no one on the island knew him, it will be days before his body is found. All right, when the police do find it, a lot of questions will be asked and they'll snoop around a bit and perhaps they won't like the look of things. But, by then, you and I will be miles away, and if they ever track us down they won't have a shred of proof he didn't die the way we're going to say he did. He tripped and fell and cracked his head against the sharp edge of a piece of furniture.' She lit her first cigarette in a long time. 'It was just one of those stupid accidents that happen to people.'

A strange new numbness had come over me and I found myself able to look at her without the least agitation of mind.

'I've ceased to care about my own future,' I said at last, 'but I can't let you do this thing. It's going to end here and now.'

I knelt in my turn beside Sacha's body. But instead of verifying for myself that he really was dead – although I had only Béa's word for it, it was no longer a matter of much consequence to me – I stretched out my hand to where his pistol had skidded, just out of reach of his grubby-nailed yet also, in the astonished dormancy of sudden death, babyish fingers.

I picked it up and checked it was loaded. Then, painfully conscious of the spectacle I was making of myself – but I couldn't have stopped now even had I wanted to – I aimed it point blank at Béa.

I saw her suck in her breath as if she had been winded. A hesitant attempt at a laugh, in which I could also detect a mocking lip-curl of incredulity, gradually gave way to a first faint inkling of real fear. Sliding out of her hand, her cigarette fell to the floor and phlegmatically smouldered on between our feet. I continued to aim at her, waiting for something to occur to me, waiting, so it felt, for my hand to tell me what to do. Then slowly, as if utterly against my will, I swung it away from Béa and towards the easel. It came to a halt only when the painting, the accursed 'Clé de Vair', was directly in the pistol's line of fire. Then I pulled the trigger. When I next looked at the canvas, I saw that it had been pierced just half an inch beneath the purse that was being transmitted from hand to hand.

It took Béa some few seconds to realise what I was doing – time for me to fire another bullet into the painting, this one winging the young nobleman and leaving a small, smoky, rip-like hole in his elegant royal-hunt waistcoat. Then she shrieked. She shrieked at me again and again to stop, fought to grab the pistol from my hand, tore at my knuckles with her fingernails, maniacally tugged at my hair. Taller than she, I waved the gun above both our heads – which meant that, when I crushed the trigger a third time, I couldn't make out if it had hit its mark. I could see only Béa's face, disfigured by fear, her eyes flicking frantically from me to the painting, back to me, then back to the painting, and I could hear only her shrieks, shrieks which were now subsiding into a shrill, weary moaning. 'Non . . . Oh non . . . non, non, non, s'il te plaît, s'il te plaît . . . Oh non . . .'

Then, as I raised the pistol again, she ripped herself from

me. She made a rush for the easel, spread her hands wide in a futile endeavour to yank the canvas off its support, turned to plead with me one last time – but it was too late. My finger had found its own undeflectable momentum and, so subtly I barely felt it move, it curled about the trigger and another explosion shook me to the core.

I had hit bull's-eye. I had hit the female figure who was furtively handing the key to her male companion. I knew I'd hit her because she screamed – because, too, before my eyes, her face began to crumble into a crazy-paving network of cracks until all at once it was obliterated by her blood. With her right hand she continued to cling to the canvas, and when she slithered to the floor she dragged both it and the easel down on top of her.

I laid Sacha's pistol on the chest of drawers, next to the candelabrum, then left the studio, closing the door behind me. I walked down the stairs and along the urine-scented hall into the medieval square which I had entered not half an hour before. Above my head the same street lamp creaked its cradle song of early-evening melancholy. There was absolutely no one to be seen. I looked at the darkening sky, from which a pale, windless mist was already rolling down the tiles of the abbey's vertiginously listing rooftop.

I started to retrace my steps through the claustrophobic little alleyway and around the lugubrious lawn. Back along the same sinuous street that Béa and I had ascended together I walked to the third of the three gates, into the same cobblestoned courtyard, then through the second gate, then the first, the tall, narrow, granite entrance carved into the ramparts, and out on to the forecourt. On that forecourt were the same symmetrically disposed parking spaces, except that, now, only the Rolls-Royce remained to be claimed.

Its door was unlocked and the keys were dangling from the dashboard: in her haste Béa had left the car without defence. I quickly got in and drove out on to the causeway.

Out on to the causeway . . . at the other end of which, as if waiting for my return, was the same sleepy village, with the same trio of parked cars still as forlorn as disused theatrical props. With a blood-red, roly-poly moon keeping pace with me for the entire length of the horizon's tightrope, I traversed the same three or four miles of flat countryside before turning on to the coastal road . . . and there, exactly where I had left it an hour before, was the same squat, phallic tower . . . there, too, always that one step ahead of me, flamboyantly underlit by the Rolls's headlamps, was the Spirit of Ecstasy, preposterous and invincible.

Suddenly, a smudge of watery white light showed up through the windscreen like an alien blip on a radar screen. It grew larger and larger. The car whose approach it was signalling to me drew closer and closer, until at last I was confronted with its lovably stumpy silhouette. It was, without any doubt at all, my own yellow second-hand Mini. Although I couldn't yet clearly make out who was in the driving seat, I knew perfectly well who it was, who it had to be.

I also knew now what *I* had to do. Coldly and calmly, just as we were about to pass each other, I jerked the steering wheel to the left. I continued to pull it left, left, left, as far as it would allow me to take it. With a nausea-inducing screech and squeal of tyres, the Rolls shot across the coastal road's central lane and bore straight down on the Mini.

This time there was no torrential rain. There was no plane tree between us. And there would be no bolt of lightning.